Red is for love, Black is for kohl

Red is for Love, Black is for kohl

PRIYANKA BHARDWAJ

LiFi Publications Pvt. Ltd.
New Delhi

Published by:
LiFi Publications Pvt. Ltd.
211, 2nd Floor, Gagandeep
12, Rajendra Place, New Delhi - 110 008, India
Phone : (011) 2574 1000
E-mail : info@lifipublications.com
Web : www.lifipublications.com

ISBN 13: 978-93-82536-09-3 ISBN 10: 93-82536-09-4

First published in 2013

Cataloging in Publication Data—DK
[Courtesy: D.K. Agencies (P) Ltd. <docinfo@dkagencies.com>]

Bhardwaj, Priyanka, 1990-
Red is for love, black is for kohl / Priyanka Bhardwaj.
p. cm.
Novel.
ISBN 9789382536093

1. Indic fiction (English) I. Title.

DDC 823.92 23

Printed in India by D.K. Fine Art Press (P) Ltd., Delhi - 52

To the woman who believed in me
more than anyone else ever will.

I miss you, Beeji.

This one is for you!

Contents

Acknowledgement

I have been planning for this part even before I had started to pen down the book. There are so many people to thank and I don't want to miss on even one.

As I start, the first person I thank with all my heart is my late grandmother Smt. Savitri Devi Bhardwaj. She spent her life waiting for that one moment when she would boast about her grand-daughter before her friends. Now that the moment is here she chose to only witness it from amongst the stars. Beeji, I cannot thank you enough for all the nourishment, nurture, faith and love!

Rohit Singh Adhikari, I thank you. For things I will never be able to express enough and for all your pathetic jokes that make no sense at all and yet lift me up from my lowest lows.

There are a few idiots who never cease to stand by me in the thick and thins of life. Thank you, Purva Chawla, Tanuj Nagpal, Disha Dhingra, Vineet Kala and Neha Chopra for everything the book is and just everything you all are! (Which is irritating, stubborn, annoying, girly and troubled in that order).

I extend my heartfelt thanks to the idiots group #2 who helped me review the various drafts, guided me and loved me all the way through. Hemani Bhandari for having loved me like a younger sister, Pulkit Chaturvedi for being my favourite boy, Raag Sarva Khullar for a yes to everything I ask for, Sahil Chopra for all the acronyms he addresses me with, Neha Choudhary for being the prime source of motivation, Kritika Malhotra, Greeshma Ramesh, Brinda Kulkarni, Piyush Deveshwar and Raj Walia, for all their encouragement, inputs and critique that shaped the plot how it is.

There are people who play significant roles in your life and mould it to something better. I thank Vinky Mam, Shipra Di, Gagandeep Singh, Sampada Sharma, Palak Jolly, Kamakshi Sharma, Bhawna Jeswani, Amit Sir, Natasha Jain, Durjoy Datta, Anant Ahuja, Ketan Gulati, Niharika Datta, Pallavie Katyal, Karishma Duggal, Himanshu Kumar, Varun Khanor, Samil Pahuja, Nikhil Bhasin, Pavi Bhasin, Ferzeen and Tanushree Mehra for having motivated me in some way or the other. Half of them have no idea about the book. They just think I have written 'something' which will get published 'somewhere'.

I thank all my friends and faculty at Bharatiya Vidya Bhavan, Daulat Ram College, Jaypee Business School and my blogger friends for their love, support and motivation.

Most importantly, I thank my publishers, LiFi Publications for having believed in me and my manuscript and I thank Rakesh Sir and Rashmi Mittal, for their unwavering guidance and co-operation.

I thank my siblings, Aditi and Virat for sparing me the fights and constant nagging whilst I was writing the book. Last but never the least I thank my family, for everything I do will always be for them and because of them.

P.S. Everybody mentioned here is to buy at least three copies of the book if not more or your name doesn't go forward to the next book, if there is one.

1

That Guy In The Street

Love. The meaning of this word has changed for me over the years. Back in grade 6, my heart raced for my co-class monitor. And ever since falling in and out of love became a usual affair until I began dating this handsome guy. Sharp, witty and not to forget cute butt! I was convinced I was finally in love. The *Twilight* love, the *A Walk to Remember* love, but I guess my Edward was still to come.

Time flew, things changed. Fights and even more fights became the mundane, and both of us knew what was impending. We broke up. A period of depression took over. My Facebook profile was overloaded with sad, lovelorn poems and notes. The world commented and cheered the 'writer', while I sulked, sitting with ice cream buckets and shed tears for everything that was a provocation of old memory. He was a nice guy, but I guess I just wasn't ready to enter a relationship then. I couldn't handle all my space being ruled by a guy alone.

"Baby, why did you not ask me before getting you hair trimmed? Sweetheart, this dress is too showy – why don't you wear something else instead? You had time to log on to Facebook, couldn't you call me if you were free? Who is that new guy on your friend list? Why does he keep liking your pictures?"

The questions never ended. My patience did.

A year went by and my single life was smooth, except for times when there were only couples all around. Even the ugliest of your friends would be dating somebody. Even that absolutely nothing girl, was dating a hunk. Well, here's a fact, when all you see are lovebirds humming, roaming, talking, performing all the 'in-a-relationship' rituals, you tend to stand before the mirror and ask yourself, "Am I that ugly?"

✦

I was in the final year pursuing a BA English (hons) at the much revered University of Delhi. Icing on the cake is getting to study in their north campus. Daulat Ram College, an all-girls college, was where I spent two years of my life and now the last one. Time flew. It seemed like only yesterday when I had filled up the admission forms.

I still remember that day when I came to campus with my parents, to fill up the forms for DU.

"Excuse me, there is a queue, if you can follow," I nudged a girl as she walked ahead of me to take the form.

"Are you the coordinator here?" she asked in a strange accent.

"Oh no, but I have brains enough to realise that following a queue makes things easy and moreover I have been sweating here in this long queue, not to let just anybody walk ahead breaking it, not to forget, with some weird American-Canadian accent," I said, my big eyes popping out.

Before she could say another word, other women too joined me and made sure she does not get her forms out of turn.

"*Beta* (child), you cannot keep messing with everyone here in Delhi like this. This is the reason why I wasn't ready to send you here for graduation," Mom rolled out in her Punjabi accent as we moved outside the college premises.

"Mom, I cannot tolerate wrong but I promise I will check my temper," I reassured her.

Worrying: mothers are awesome at this.

My family is like any other Punjabi family. Mom, Dad, Arjun *Bhaiya*, my elder brother, Mishti, my younger sister, *Beeji,* my grandmother and *Bauji,* my grandfather.

Our vocal chords were a little more blessed than others. While we could not lay claims to the family of the great Ustads of Lucknow, we could certainly imagine sharing some vocal kinship or connection with Dolly Bindra!

We talk across rooms to each other from the farthest ends of the house. That's not shouting, is it?

We lived in Jalandhar, Punjab. Convincing my family to send me to Delhi for graduation wasn't tough, really. It took a series of hunger fasts and agitations, days when I wouldn't stop crying, frequent cajoling and persuasion by *Bhaiya*, Mishti, neighbours, their neighbours, relatives, their relatives, the maid, watchman, milkman, the newspaperman, and so many others. Until, they finally agreed.

Mishti, in those days, was preparing for her twelfth board exams. *Bhaiya* had just completed his MBA from North Carolina

University and returned home after his work placement here. Since then, Mom was ever so eager to get him hitched, as he had begun earning. This was the benchmark for marriage eligibility in India today.

"*Beta*, Chopra ji's daughter is really pretty, you must see her. She is a teacher in DPS," Mom would say to him.

And the same suggestion was modified to replace Chopra ji's daughter with Khurana ji's, Khanna ji's and Bhardwaj ji's.

Bhaiya would react by turning up the television volume high or simply leaving the room, because getting into arguments with Mom is useless! Moms have the expertise and charm to win. No wonder dad never said a thing on the matter.

✦

Delhi welcomed me with open arms. A city that was too beautiful and full of life, though not safe in the nights. A universal threat of antisocial elements made it an alarming place to live. But I quickly learnt how to adapt.

It was a long day at college and a boring one too, for only a few of my friends turned up. There were only two lectures and I had an assignment deadline to meet too. As I walked back to my flat in Vijay Nagar right next to the campus, which I shared with my friend Niti, something unexpected happened. Unaccustomed as I still am, to crossing the Delhi roads alone to the unrelenting flow of traffic, I had barely crossed the road when a car screeched to a halt inches away from my feet. My heart did a somersault.

People were walking in slow motion, a dupatta had flown in with the breeze wrapped across my face with *DDLJ* music in the background, I was shot a glimpse of a 6′1″ frame of dark, handsome man with slight stubble, muscular build in white shirt, gray trousers walking towards me. My heart raced about, lost.

"I am very sorry. I was rushing for a meeting. I had just joined office and I didn't want to be late for this one. I hope you didn't get hurt," he said.

"Umm… No… Err…," was all I could utter with much effort.

I was hypnotised. He apologised again and turned to leave. I quickly took to my heels. I walked a few steps but the guy's vision remained with me. My thoughts were all over the place, when a horn blared into my ears from behind. Was it him again? I would have died of heart failure. Too much hotness, too much warming.

It was him who rolled down his window to say again,"And pardon me this, but you have very beautiful eyes," he smiled as I blushed.

Off he rode and took my heart with him. I was in love. Yes, love all over again. Only, if I could see him one more time, I would tell him he was beyond awesome.

I don't know if I would ever see him but I was in love again for at least sometime now and it felt good.

I reached the flat. Niti was asleep.

"Get up biatch, daddy is home," I said removing the bed sheet.

"Hey dad! How was the day at college?" she said still covering her face with the pillow.

"Nothing about the college but you have to listen what happened on my way back home, get up get up get up," I said shaking her.

"Fuck off Naina, let me sleep! It's not as if you met the man of your dreams on the streets," she murmured irritated.

"Exactly biatch!" I shouted with a grin.

She immediately got up, excited.

"What?"she asked puzzled.

I told her about the road incident and her smile widened as she listened.

"Aww! That is so cute! You are a lucky bitch! Why do all the hot and handsome guys have to fall prey to you," she said making a face.

"Because your spaces are already occupied by books," I said.

"Ya whatever," she said.

Niti was the nerd amongst us. She was the class topper. A night before exams, I would just ask her to blabber all about the subject and I would not just pass but score reasonably well. Such was Niti's talent, or rather mine! And mind you, it just didn't take this to pass the exams. A lot more was required, for instance, a bed. While Niti would speak and I would lie down and listen. Anyway, she was very hardworking, unlike me.

✦

The next day in college was fun. The freshers had joined their classes and we seniors were ready to rag them. Though ragging was banned, a little fun in the name of introduction was acceptable. Freshers wouldn't complain to the teachers out of fear of being teased by the seniors for the rest of their time in the college.

I entered the English hons. 1st year classroom with Niti and some of our classmates. A huge class it was. The college had taken in almost 70 girls under the course. The expressions we encountered were of fear, depression, nervousness and some constipated looks too. But there was one face amongst the rest that stood out, as chilled out as we were. Though all of them tried very hard to present smiling faces, her smile was genuine and it reflected in her eyes. It was decided, she was the one to rag first.

"Hi girls, we are your super seniors, the third years. There is no need to feel scared. We are here just for some fun and interaction with you guys," I announced.

All of them smiled. And then we introduced ourselves one by one to them. Done with this, we called her out.

"The one in the black sleeveless top there, yes you. We would like to start the introduction session with you and then will follow a talent round which shall be at your ease. If you don't want to go about it, we won't force you and this holds for everybody,"said Niti.

She came down till the podium and started, "Hi, I am Isha Bhandari," and rest of her introduction followed.

"So Isha, you want to present something on your own or you want us to ask something of you," I asked.

"Whatever you say should be good," she said confidently.

"All right then, you are in wrong hands babe," I said teasing her. "You will now have to consider anyone here the pole and perform a pole dance for us."

"Can I have the liberty of considering you as the pole?" she hit back.

Isha! Isha! Isha! – The crowd had broken into raptures and it was all that I could hear! Suddenly, the constipated crowd seemed to have swallowed Hajmola and now looked like a lynch mob at some playboy party. We played Britney Spears' 'Gimme More'. What followed next were some hot moves by her on an embarrassed me; I had never felt so shy in my entire life. Shy, because she was so hot and seductive that had I been a boy I would have taken her home.

"I hope you didn't mind," said Isha once she was done.

"I didn't, though I would have loved it had I been a boy," I said winking.

Both of us laughed and then hugged.

She has been my favourite since then. Confident and sexy with her head firm on her shoulders. Then followed introductions with the rest of the class. We told them about the upcoming freshers' event in the college and left.

It seemed a nice, bright and friendly batch. Amongst us seniors, Isha was the universal favourite. I smiled for having found a new friend in her. There was a connection I felt, a good one.

✦ ✦ ✦

2

As I Save The Day

While I still was in love-at-first-sight mode for this absolutely out-of-the-world charming man, Niti was getting all panicky about the freshers' event that was to be held in the college very soon. She was the college president. For the first two years in college, she numbed my ears with her wish list. A long one. From one to hundred, her first and last wish remained "wants to become the college president". Although my bestie, Niti could really get on your nerves when she panicked! Too impulsive, I always asked her to be less dramatic and less hyper.

"Babe, I am so screwed, the sponsors, the judges nothing has been finalized, you haven't taken the auditions, teachers are least interested, the juniors are hardly responsible, how will I manage the event alone like this, I just cannot handle so much responsibility alone, someone has to take an initiative… lalalala," and she didn't stop until I lied,"Stop! I just peed in my pants."

She shut up.

This event was scheduled to be a beauty pageant contest to select a 'Miss Daulat Ram College' every year. I was going to be the proud choreographer of this event. Pretty freshers would catwalk and be judged on their talent and wits.

Being in an all-girls' college was an experience to remember. While the first few months were a challenge having studied in a co-ed school for some 13 years of my life and suddenly all around me seeing nothing but women, things got better after we realised life was not all that sad without boys. A girls' college has its own charm and fun. We would sometimes seduce each other like in a strip club and that's a sight I bet no boy would want to miss. Also, now and then you observed butts moving, how big whose boobs were and also sometimes mushy gay couples in the girl's common room and front lawns. But this does not mean I am homosexual. For all the boys who read this, I have a straight orientation, please. Even if, the only male figure who caught my attention in the college was the canteen guy. He would take the token with a wide grin on his face and would get my order at the earliest possible.

Every time he got me my order, I would smile and say "thank you" and he would blush more and smile adorably!

We didn't even have any male teachers, though some were expected. The administrative staff was full of uncles except one. Ajay Jamwal. He was indeed eye candy for all the girls and teachers. Many girls would intentionally throw their ID cards away so that they could go, do office rounds and in the quest for a duplicate ID card would seize a sight of Ajay sir! And yes, Niti did this too. I still tease her with his name.

Anyway, coming back to the event, it took a week to start and I got busy taking auditions to select the candidates. You could really recognize a fresher from the face. The zeal to feel the part of the crowd, though with a slight apprehension, the uber-cool bags and garments and the way they would don their glasses! The *fucchas,* as we called them, were all keen to take part in the event. There would be a huge line outside the girl's common room for the auditions. Niti was busy arranging judges and sponsors for the event and I got busy taking the auditions. The candidates were shortlisted and the list was put up. The practices began from the very next day at the centre stage of the college. There would be a huge crowd of girls at the centre stage and the parapets of the floors witnessing the practice sessions. It would really give a kick to the morale of the contestants and well yes, I felt great! I was the boss!

"Girls, move your butts and follow the line. Feel like a girl and not man for god's sake."

I was heard shouting these all the time.

The day of the event had come. We had a number of sponsors and a big shot judging panel this year. Niti was indeed the best college president we have had so far. I was so proud of her.

"Who all are in the judging panel?" I asked one of the juniors.

"Rishab Reddy, a designer-engineer, Bharti Taneja from Alps, lecturer from the college besides last year's Ms. DRC," she said.

"Is this Rishab Reddy hot? Is he straight?" I asked her.

"Ha-ha, anyway, Niti *di* (didi) is looking for you," she said giggling and went. And I kept wondering what was so funny about what I had said.

The Engineer-Designer thing sounded strange to me. I have seen a lot of engineers taking up writing novels but then a designer, this was something peculiarly… Ehh… Weird!

Niti asked me to receive him at the college gate while boasting about his looks and demeanour but I was least interested, so I sent a few juniors.

The event commenced with Niti's welcome note and was in full swing – women hooting for women, drooling over women hitting the ramp; this was an outlandish sight to be seen in a girl's college alone. And believe me, it's not all that bad.

The talent round started next. I saw Niti running towards me.

"Naina, the CD player isn't working. Shit, what are we going to do now?" she panicked.

"Don't worry Niti, let's see what can we do about it," I said trying to calm her down.

The gap fillers were done, and the crowd was getting restless. I saw Niti on the verge of tears.

"Look Niti, arrange for someone's laptop and speakers and meanwhile I will just see what I can do," I said.

She left with a couple of girls and I called up Priyanka, the head of Debonair, the fashion society of our college.

"Hey Priyanka, Naina here. Listen, can you and your girls walk any of your themes right now on the stage? There is a problem with the CD player," I asked.

"I can never say no to you Naina. Give me five minutes and I will come with my girls," she said. My connections never disappointed me.

In no time, those ten most gorgeous girls of the college draped some dupattas and did an exceptional theme number which they called 'Naturally in Love'.

They performed well and swayed everyone's hearts. This was apparent from the 'once mores' erupting from the crowd.

"You know, had you been a boy I would have made out with you RIGHT NOW!!!" Niti said with a wide grin on her face.

"Oooohh, classroom sex, sounds amazing! How I wish I were a boy," I said with a sad face.

We did not realise but everyone was by then staring at us and broke into laughter as I said that.

I was happy that I had saved the day. The laptop was arranged and the event moved on smoothly.

Following this, I was called on to the stage to be given the thank you memento.

"I request our drop dead gorgeous choreographer Naina Shergil to please come over the stage and walk the ramp for us," called out the compère.

The moment I entered the stage, the crowd broke into raptures of 'Naina Naina Naina'. While I was walking on the ramp I saw something in the front row that seemed familiar. But I could hardly make out.

"I request all the judges to please come over the stage and announce the much awaited result," announced the compère.

I couldn't believe what my eyes saw. The same guy who had struck me between the roads the other day, yes, that same 6′1″, tall handsome guy, was one of the judges?! Rishab Reddy, the engineer cum designer?! Holy cow! Was destiny playing her games around me?!

I went to Niti and cried out loud, "You ass, this Rishab Reddy is the same guy whom I was talking about that day. That hot guy who was about to first kill me by his car but then he had killed me by his looks."

"Eww, the last line was creepy," she said.

"Can you shut up and tell me why you didn't tell me about him," I asked panicking.

"So how in the world will I know of the same. Now let me manage the wrapping up of the event and by the way, you didn't even go to receive him when I asked you to, so, you A-s-s," she said.

And I didn't go to receive him; I could have died the very moment and cursed my over analyses of people and things. Only if my imagination was less wild. And he looked even handsome in a suit. Grey suit with a white shirt, my favourite combination! Now the only thing I prayed for was that he shouldn't be a gay. I would have landed into a similar trauma I was in, when I got to know of Neil Patrick Harris (Barney Stinson) being a gay. I mean how a guy, who was a complete Casanova over the screen and who would take every second woman to bed without even knowing her name could possibly be a gay?

"Oh my God! He is so hot," whispered a few juniors, drooling.

"Only if I could take him home," said another.

Girls, I tell you are even hornier than boys these days.

Niti meanwhile came and whispered in my ear,"Did Tanya tell you he is a gay?"

Tanya was our neighbour and a classmate. But my biggest fear had come true, he was a gay and I made a long face looking nowhere.

"Oh! I felt likewise, most designers are gay after all," I said.

"Designer? He is doing his engineering!" said Niti.

"He is through with his engineering, did you go deaf while the compère was announcing this," I said.

"Even the compère knows stuff about him now?" she asked shocked.

"The whole college knows by now, so what? Judge's profile is a must to be announced."

"Judge? Who the hell are you talking about?"

"Rishab Reddy."

"Oh get over him Naina! I was talking about Tanya's crush, he is a gay. And that is why he didn't show any interest in Tanya but all in her brother,"she said.

I would have kissed Niti in her lips for having said that. I felt so relieved. I was just hoping that Rishab shouldn't be a gay now. I prayed. I literally did.

✦ ✦ ✦

3

The Pursuit Of The Number

It was long now that I had waited and prayed for Rishab to have a straight orientation. I had kept my fingers crossed. I didn't want him to be gay. But nothing could have clicked between me and this celebrity engineer-designer or whatever, anyway. He would have even forgotten by now about the almost road accident thing, I thought. Well, I stood afar admiring the charm of this absolutely sexy man. I was waiting for this Greek God of a man to hold the mic and declare "Naina Shergil, I love you too." Yea, one of my many random fantasies concerning him that time. And one of very decent ones too. He took up the mic. "Well it has been a great pleasure… lalala… Naina Shergil… lalala… Great choreography… lalala… Would love to… lalala," was all I managed to grasp. I quickly googled his name and thankfully no particular searches revealed any bisexual traits in him.

I was happy at least, I thought, I had fallen for a straight guy. I didn't want to be another Konkona Sen Sharma, whose love interest in almost every movie turns out to be gay. Anyway, while the event was winding up, those juniors of mine were all set to see him off and I was on my toes trying to seize the opportunity first. I quickly called them.

"Umm… You guys had refreshments?" I inquired.

"Yes," they said.

"And you have given refreshments to the contestants too?"

"No," they said their faces dripping with lust and lust alone as they seized glimpses of Rishab.

"Girls?!!! What are you doing, go get going and manage the refreshments department," I ordered.

"But we were about to see Mr. Rishab Reddy off. You had asked us to do that, you remember?"

"So does that mean you will not comply with other responsibilities? Get going and handle the refreshment allocation to the candidates now," I said firmly.

"Now I will have see off Mr. Reddy myself, phew! You guys can get so careless at times," and this is how I grind my own axe! I winked at myself and went where Rishab Reddy was standing.

"Hey," I said.

"Hey, hi … So we meet again," he remarked.

I was even more in love now. He remembers me!

"I thought you might not retain the memory of the day," I said.

"I might have forgotten the day, maybe your face, but how can someone forget those eyes, once again, they are bewitching," he said.

I was swaying, man! Tremors went down my spine. Like really. He was a charmer indeed. We walked towards the gate and he gave me his card.

"Hope to hear from you soon," he said and left. I was dumbstruck by his last statement and gesture.

✦

I went back to Niti and told her everything.

"You lucky bitch," she said and hugged me.

"So what are the plans like? You guys going around soon it seems," she said.

"There is nothing cooking babes, we have just met and we don't even know each other that well," I said.

"As if a guy has to know you to fall for you, aren't these eyes enough to cast the spell of love," she said.

I loved her all the more in times like these. She was one hell of an ego booster.

"Awwwww," I said and hugged her.

We went home after a coffee and dark temptation at Barista sponsored by Niti alone. This was a treat for me for having saved the day. Dark Temptation was something I could live my whole life on: a warm chocolate cake oozing with hot chocolate syrup with whipped cream and a tight scoop of Vanilla ice cream on the side. The moment it touched my lips I closed my eyes, savouring it to the core. It was like having multiple orgasms in a go. And suddenly I felt great about being a woman.

We went back home around eight and were too tired to prepare dinner. We were in our beds to sleep and then I realised *'Hum aapke hain kaun'* was to be telecast on Zee Cinemas. We couldn't have missed that. It was our favourite movie. There have been times when we would mute the sound and iterate the dialogues as the movie played.

We quickly switched the television on and after watching it, crashed into our beds. I took out Rishab's visiting card wondering how to go about it. I started fiddling with it and right in front of my eyes everything played out as if in a movie. The first time I met him, and then the moment he praised my eyes TWICE, walking down to the college gate with him, everything was so beautiful and cute. I didn't realise when in the midst of all this I had fallen asleep.

The next morning I got up pretty late and missed some lectures. Niti had already left. She would never miss any of the lectures and I would hardly make it to them.

The room looked clean to me. The maid had done the house already. I looked around for the card Rishab gave me. F**k! It wasn't around! I checked in the bin, it wasn't there too. I quickly called up Niti to ask if she had kept it safe. The ring tone was set to some cheesy Bollywood love song. I thought I must have dialled a wrong number and so I quickly disconnected the call. I called again, and again the same song rang. What was Niti thinking while she set this as her caller tune? Now this was important for me to know. Like a matter of life and death.

She answered the call and I started shouting, "What in the world were you thinking when you set this caller tune?"

"*Arre*, these mobile service providers you know, I don't know how it became my caller tune," she said.

"So? What are you waiting for, get rid of this now," I said.

"They have charged me bloody 30 bucks for this one, let me at least exploit it to its value," she retorted.

"You will let this remain your caller tune because you want to avail of the value of your 30 chips? You miser!" I yelled. "Take 50 from me and get rid of this thing."

"70 it is. Deal?" she said.

"You are disgusting. Anyway, tell me fast, did you see Rishab Reddy's business card around in the room or flat?" I asked irritably.

"No," she said and I disconnected the call before she could say anything else.

I thought I was devastated. The world seemed to have come to an end. I had lost the only chance to talk to the one guy who looked amazingly handsome, was a celebrity and who possibly wanted to talk to me too. Super! I congratulated myself for this and lay down on my bed. After I restored myself, I thought of ways to find a solution. I looked for his contact details in Google. But to my sorrow, there was none except for a couple of email IDs. I was in grief. My phone suddenly rang, it was Isha.

"Hey Isha," I answered the call.

"Hey *Di*, I am downstairs with Mohit. He landed yesterday from Bangalore. I wanted you to meet him, come fast," she said.

"Oh that's great, you come over here. We will have lunch together," I said.

"We are in a hurry *Di*, come down NOW," she said authoritatively.

"Isha come over, no! Not feeling too elated. Sit for half an hour please," I pleaded and it worked.

Mohit was Isha's boyfriend. These kids were too much in love. The bell rang.

"Heyyyyyyy," I shrieked and Isha and I hugged each other.

"Hi, Mohit," I said and shook his hand.

"Not bad, *haan*," I said while I looked at Isha and nudged her. She blushed and nudged me. Mohit was really very handsome and they looked amazingly cute together.

"Ok, so you guys sit here meanwhile I will get some coffee and cookies," I said.

"Mohit, you must not miss out on the world's best coffee," she said.

"She is just being kind Mohit, she loves me too much," I said with a smile. "By the way, you guys are allowed to get naughty while I am in the kitchen, there is nobody in here," I winked and went.

✦

The coffee gave way to a discussion over politics and a gossip session. Isha and I would always discuss politics without fail. This was a topic that always gave us an adrenaline rush.

She found me a little lost unlike the other times we discussed this and asked me what was bothering me. I told her the whole episode and I don't know what made her caution me with, "*Di*, you can act really dumb at times."

"Why?" I asked.

"Why don't you ask Niti *di*? She is the president and she must know his number," she said.

Now I understand why she said that I felt like a fool. And I would have kissed Isha too.

Suddenly I realised a lot of girls are making me feel like this, first Niti, then Isha.

"*Di* you may now resume your mission: Find Rishab's number and we shall leave, it's been quite a while now," she said.

I hugged them bye and texted her. *Thanks baby and you two look adorable together. Tell him if he ever thinks of cheating on you it should be because of me, *wink*.*

This was a ritual. You are supposed to text your friends immediately after you meet their boyfriends/girlfriends.

I was back to my own self now.

What the hell was I thinking? My best friend is the president of the college and she must be having Rishab's number as she is the one who called him for judging. Bull's eye! This was no rocket science but I lose my sanity when panic stricken. I must have acquired this from Niti, I thought.

I called her again. I wasn't in a mood to torture myself with that caller tune, but then, Rishab was important and then I dialled and ended up listening to that Bollywood song once again. She didn't answer the call. I tried once more and the song continued.

She disconnected the call and texted: *In lecture, this will continue for the next three hours. Talk to you later.*

I couldn't have waited for so long, but then was there another option? I tried to divert my mind but to my dismay, nothing worked; those three hours seemed like centuries to me. I waited.

✦ ✦ ✦

4

When Niti Kisses Me

I checked the time for like, the 100th time. Still an hour to go. I thought of torturing myself a bit more, so I called up Niti again to hear that caller tune.

She disconnected the phone and I sensed her irritation. She hated being disturbed during lectures. A text came my way, "What the hell do you think you are doing? Just hide your ass somewhere before I break it into four."

Had she been here I know how exactly she must have looked, all boiled up, flaring nostrils and shouting. She would only hold her tongue when I would announce, "The hair inside your nose are poking out." She would deliver an ugly expression that made her look only cuter.

I loved teasing her.

I hid my phone under the pillow and switched on the television. NDTV 24X7 showed visuals of the Mumbai blasts. They were gross images from the blast sites. I flipped the channel to look for something peppy so as to lift up my mood. *Emotional atyachaar* was next with a girl sobbing over her infidel boyfriend. Next, some *saas-bahu* soap. There were a lot of Ekta Kapoors in the market now, I thought and before I felt claustrophobic, I changed the channel. I thought some music on NTV should be good, but to my dismay they showed weirdly dressed girls pulling each other's hair on some silly issues. Useless and the most dumb programme I have ever seen.

After checking the time again when the lecture was expected to be over, I called her up and the woman answered almost immediately.

"Are you out of your mind? I was sitting just ahead of Ms. Veera Khanna and you know how strict she is, how in the world can you go on calling me like that when you know she doesn't really like me, in the first place?" she shouted.

"Your hair is poking out of your nose," I said.

"Shut up and tell me what do you want?" she asked.

"You look so cute when angry," I said to tease her more.

"Really? You are going to find me adorable in no time," she said. "Will you tell me what you want," she shouted and I grinned.

"Do you have Rishab's phone number?" I asked.

"Who Rishab?" she asked.

"Your dad dumb wit, I am going around with him,"I said angrily.

"Hey step-mom, you won't beat me and then leave me and mom in the streets right?" she said nasally.

"I would spank your ass with a rod," I said angrily.

"Ooh! That sounds erotic," she said.

"Niti please ya! Tell me if you have his number," I begged.

"Yes I do, and it's even there in your phone. I had saved it there because you know my phone memory keeps giving up," she said.

"You are such a bitch but I love you anyway," I exclaimed disconnecting the call.

The whole morning I was looking for a number which was right there in my phone. Awesome, I thought. And there it was, a number in bright black, bold letters that read Rishab Reddy, dreamy! I stared at the number and smiled for a few minutes, when the doorbell rang. It was a post for Niti. I received and kept it aside. I was too lovesick to notice anything but the number on my phone.

I thought of calling him, but then I had to talk to Niti and discuss first. Moreover he must have been busy then, I thought. It will be appropriate if I call him in the evening. I settled for an afternoon nap and Niti woke me up around dusk.

"Hey, you're back," I asked.

"No, it's my ghost, I will get into your body and make out with Rishab Reddy," she said.

"Oh get into me fast then baby," I said and both of us hi-fived and laughed.

I gave her the mail that had come for her. She opened it and after a few minutes tears trickled down her cheeks. I was worried. I asked her whose letter it was.

"Who sends letters dumb wit, I own a mobile phone," she said.

Yea, she was right. I don't know what made me ask her that, I was too worried perhaps. But then writing letters was like a ritual in my family. Just for the dose of some fun, Mom would write letters to me. She wasn't any less dramatic.

Cool, I wasn't all that silly when I asked Niti of that. I made a mental note.

"I am selected for the Ernst and Young internship, for these Diwali vacations. I thought I won't make it. It is such a revered place. I so wanted it and it's here in my hand," she said with excitement.

"So why the hell were you crying," I asked annoyed.

"Happy tears idiot," she said with a grin.

I shrugged. Like I told you, the super dramatic her. Why on earth was all the drama happening around me all the time, making my life so filmy?

"Niti, tell me how to go about the Rishab Reddy thing, man. I am getting all nervous," I said fidgeting with the cell phone.

"Naina, call him now you crazy woman! Guys should sweat when they see you and not the other way round," she said.

"So should I be calling him?" I asked.

"Right away!!!" ordered Niti.

I called him, and the ringtone sounded *look into my eyes, you will see* from Bryan Adams' 'Everything I do, I do it for you' song. Both of us were like, "Awwwwwwww, so cute," and giggled.

This was my favourite song; I had always imagined my perfect kiss to happen with this playing in the background. Anyway, though I was nervous about calling him, Niti was my strength, and I had her by my side, so it was all good. He answered the call with, "Hello?"

Something strange went through me and I kept the phone down. Shivers ran down my spine. His baritone was orgasmic, even over the phone. Niti chided me for being faint-hearted. I never thought of myself that way.

"Are you the same Naina, talking to whom, boys would pee in their pants?" she asked.

"Shut up Niti, he was too hot to handle," I said.

And my phone rang, and *Rishab Reddy calling* flashed. Niti snatched the phone from my grip and took the call before handing it to me.

"Hello," I found myself saying.

"Umm, I just had a call from this number," said Rishab.

"Err...," I stuttered as Niti poked me to speak.

Here I was, trying to speak to this man, but all that my vocal chords managed was an "err". An 'err' all over again? From the first time in the street to now, an err. Hopeless, I thought. *Throw more words out of my mouth*, I shouted in silence.

I took a deep breath, collected all my guts and spoke, "Hi, Naina this side."

"Naina Shergil?" he inquired.

"Yea, so how have you been? Oh by the way, I hope I haven't disturbed you by any chance?" I asked.

"Hey! Hi... No no not at all, how have you been? And what took you so long to call? See I was just too embarrassed for that road accident thing so I just wanted to take you out for dinner, lunch or coffee whatever is good with you. That's just my way of apologizing and please don't deny," he said immediately.

"Pretty much to the point, *haan*," Niti murmured.

Shut up Niti, I warned silently, my cheeks flushing red.

"That's just too sweet of you Rishab but this isn't needed at all, it's all good," I said.

"I know, I know, you are too kind but then just for my peace of mind and maybe I can, for an evening boast around, pretending to date the prettiest girl ever," he said.

Now what do you say to something like this? I was bowled over by this one. I said yes right away and after exchanging a few words, we hung up for he was driving home. He lived in Greater Kailash alone. His parents lived in Bahrain.

It was decided that we meet at Connaught Place, for picking me up would have been too tiresome for him as my house was on a different route altogether. We were to meet over the weekend for a coffee in the evening and that happened to be the next day.

I kept the phone down and joined Niti to shout at the pitch of our voices, "AAAAAAAAAAAAAAAAAA!"

We were ecstatic! We went mad! Booze was sure to flow, to celebrate this one. I was going out for coffee with an almost celebrity, super sexy and cute guy! This was sure a dream.

✦

Niti and I got ready and left for Khan Market in the evening, for Café Route 04. We had a double reason to celebrate: her internship and my love blossoming. The crowd there was always hot and we were ready to make heads turn! I wore my halter top and green skirt, left my hair open and followed my sexy eye ritual – kohl, and a lot of kohl. It was almost as if I painted my eyes with it. Getting ready for me meant nothing without kohl. I knew I could pull off the ugliest of pyjamas if you just let me paint my eyes with the kohl. Silver earrings and big golden and silver *kadas* (bangles), I was done for the night.

Niti dressed up in her favourite black *kurti* (a short kurta). She was more than elated today. Actually, we both were.

"Baby you look sexy and this tattoo at your bare shoulder peeking out to grab attention is melting my heart and your big eyes with thick lashes and kohl is making me drool," she said like a boy, now holding my waist.

"Thanks love and you look okay," I said teasingly.

"Bitch," she said with that weird expression she usually makes and we got moving.

We boarded the metro from Vishwa Vidyalaya metro station, got down at Rajeev Chowk and took an auto for Khan Market. We asked the auto-wallah to stop a little ahead of our destination, for we didn't want to be seen alighting an auto rickshaw amongst those who got out from Audis and BMWs. And at times like these, we would fervently promise each other and ourselves that we would make it big in life one day to enjoy all this and more.

As soon as we reached the café, oh boy, all heads turned! But not because we looked amazingly out of the world, which I'm sure we sure did, but because a waiter had just bumped into Niti, spilling dirty cocktails all over her *kurti*. I could have killed him, the ass had spoilt my baby's favourite *kurti*. But she was calm, as always. Her anger was useless for she would only take it out on me once we got home.

"I… I am very sorry Ma'am," he apologised.

And before I could say anything, our tender Niti replied, "Oh, that's ok, it happens."

She went to the washroom, cleaned her *kurti* and joined me after a while. We ordered nachos and burritos with vodka shots. We had to celebrate, so shots were definitely the call of the day!

The order came, and nachos and burritos were put aside so that we could concentrate more on the shots.

One down, two, three, four, five and she gave up. I greedily continued with the sixth and the seventh one too!

We were drunk, at least I was. We giggled and talked so loudly, as if we owned the café. Later we went to the nearby CCD lounge to down some espresso shots to sober up.

"You know what Niti baby, I would always think that love wasn't meant for me. I wasn't too good handling the last one you know, I almost thought that this love saga ends for me here, and then this guy comes to my life," I said.

"Aww baby, don't say like that. You are every boy's dream. Milky white baby soft skin, silky shiny hair which look even hot when wet, pink little lips, big black eyes with thick lashes shouting for attention and not to forget your sexy curves, who wouldn't want to fall in love with you?" she said bolstering me.

"Niti? You sure have a straight orientation, right?" I said.

"You are ugly Naina, in the true sense of it," she uttered with a straight face.

"See, not everyone thinks likewise," I said and she immediately hugged me as we laughed.

"Awayyyyyy, people are watching. I don't want to throw wrong hints at them," I cautioned.

Through her ways of hugging and kissing me, she made it quite obvious for people to think we were into each other. I hated her for this. A super cute guy who was staring at me all the while when we were in some resto-bar a few days back, left the place after Niti hugged me and kissed me in the public the way she does.

We had our coffee shots and left for home. We reached somewhere around 11 and Niti dozed off right away. Insomnia was bothering me, for the very next day I was to meet Rishab. What to wear, what was going to happen, how will he greet me, should I just shake hands or hug, all this was hovering over my mind and I just couldn't sleep. Dogging from one side to the other, fiddling with the pillow I spent the night.

I went to the terrace after the clock struck four and in no time the scene stupefied me. Sunrise, they have always said is even better a sight than the Seven Wonders of the World. I knew what awaited me. The day when I would unravel the lover in me one more time. The day to ascertain how it hits off with Rishab, the beginning of the day was beautiful indeed; I was just hoping for the end to be even more consummating.

✦ ✦ ✦

5

Another Guy In The Streets

Yes, I definitely was excited to meet him. Happy, but not the kind of ecstatic I thought I would be. Something lacked. Maybe I was scared all over again for a new start. I don't know what it was. I was unable to confine it to words, so I let it pass. I would ponder over it later, I thought.

It was nine in the morning and we were to meet around four. I woke Niti up.

"Good morning sweety! All geared up for the big day?" she asked in a super elated, dizzy tone.

"Yea yea, I was wondering what to wear. Get up and help me out," I said.

We got finished with the breakfast and sat before the wardrobe. A huge pile of clothes stared at us in the face. I would never arrange my wardrobe. Niti would always do that for me. And it had been quite some time since she did it last time, for we were busy with the Ms. DRC event. She was my darling. These three years vanished in thin air and I already know how much I am to cry when we would leave for our post-graduation. We had different plans. She wanted to do MBA and I wanted to do Mass Communication. We would promise each other of keeping together and teaching each other's kids English and Maths.

Anyway, even after having tried everything on, from her clothes to mine, from the ones we borrowed from Tanya, our classmate and neighbour, who had an average sense of styling, none of the clothes ended up getting a heads up.

When it came to me and Niti, we hardly loved anyone else's dressing acumen over ours. Narcissists, we were.

"Babe, I don't have any clothes," I said.

"Oho when do you say otherwise?" she said making a face.

"Now are you going to tell me what to do?" I asked.

"Let's hit K-nags, you will be able to source a dress from that new store 'Delhi to London',"she suggested. K-nags is the Delhi University lingo for Kamla Nagar market which was adjacent to the north campus and opposite Hans Raj College.

"Umm, yes OK, move your ass," I said hurrying.

We changed our tees, slipped into shorts and left for K-nags. Tanya saw us heading out. She lived in the flat right above ours. She asked if she could join us and we had to say yes. We hopped into a rickshaw and quickly got going. A car with loud music crossed us and we knew this must be some wannabe stud! It was honking right behind us. Irritated, I called the man out and asked the rickshaw-wallah to stop. Niti and Tanya knew the man had speed-dialled trouble.

A huge man, with two upper shirt buttons open and chest hair not just peeking out, but all over, hopped out of the car.

"What's wrong with you? Seeing girls for the first time or what? Can't you just drive your car right and get going?" I questioned, angrily.

"The length of your clothes drove me to your legs baby than driving the car," he said fingering his chest hair. Gross.

I don't know what went through me, but I caught the man by his collar and slapped him right across his face. People had already gathered around. He couldn't collect himself again realising what had happened. I threatened him to hold his ears and apologise in front of everyone (yes, I do that if people mess with ethics) or I would take him to the nearby police station. He, of course, had no way of escape, as there were a lot of people around, who were angry at the bloody nuisance caused by him. Ashamed, he left.

"I am so proud of you, sweety!"said Niti and smiled.

"Well done! Girls must never tolerate if goons like him go out of hand," a lady said patting my shoulder.

"Indeed aunty," I said and smiled.

I felt so proud of myself. I have always believed that tolerating nuisance only further abets the problem.

Back on the rickshaw, Tanya spoke in her ever-so-nasal twang, "You should have just ignored it. He might be some local goon or something. At least he looked like one."

"And this does nothing but encourages dick-heads," I retorted.

"Now he'll think twice before doing that to any other girl. Wearing short clothes is not an open invite to any jackass to go messing around," added Niti.

We reached the store and I quickly grabbed a *kurti*. I thought of wearing something ethnic. A black plain *kurti* with noodle straps caught my eye. We quickly took it and Tanya remained in the market for her boyfriend to come and see her. He was some guy from the NSUI, the student political body of DU. After the trauma of her previous crush who had turned out to be gay, Tanya declared she was seeing a new guy. Somewhere down the line, we met him with Tanya. I really felt odd about his personality on the first meeting itself. He was wearing red shoes with yellow laces (read on!) and his tri coloured jeans (still more to come!) had a chain hanging around his waist. A chain? Yes! Anyway, you must have by now understood, how handsome and chic he was.

It was three o'clock in the afternoon. An hour to go and we were still in the market. We immediately rushed home and I started getting ready. A good thirty minutes and I was done.

The black *kurti* and churidaar with a red Jaipuri dupatta and Kolhapuris. I left my hair loose and put a small black bindi. My favourite silver earrings, watch and kohl, which was a part and parcel of my eyes by now. I was ready.

"You look wonderful," said Niti and tried the guys' whistle for the n-th time.

I knew I had done wonders. I carry off the ethnic stuff best. But I looked exceptionally great that day. I poured my favourite Burberry cologne and picked up my clutch.

My phone rang. Rishab Reddy calling.

"Hey," I said.

"Hey, I am leaving for CP. Have you left?" he asked.

"Oh yes, I will be leaving soon," I said.

I quickly checked myself from top to bottom and hugged Niti.

"All the luck sweety," she said excitedly.

I had called a cab and reached CP in a good thirty minutes. He was very much on time and asked me to get down at Palika Bazaar's gate number one. I saw beautiful tall buildings, people walking down the busy roads, the steady flow of transport, and then him. I quickly spotted Rishab, who wore a nice grey and white striped shirt and beige trousers, looking handsome as always. We greeted each other with a handshake.

"Naina, you look really pretty. And the bindi looks amazing on you," he said smiling.

I blushed and thanked him.

"So where do we go? QBA?" he asked.

"Can we go somewhere that is more commonplace? Barista or Costa?" I said.

He looked at me, smiled and then said yes.

We walked until we found a newly opened café. I had butterflies in my stomach. You know that feeling when you are smiling, smiling and SMILING? Yaaa… THAT!

"So why Connaught Place? We could have gone to Saket! CP is always so crowded," he said, as we walked along the inner circle.

"We people make the crowd and that's what I love about CP. This place is so full of life. One place I can never get enough of. The inner circle, the central park, tall buildings which looked even more beautiful while lit during the night, the wide roads, parliament house, the India Gate, everything would just strike the right chords within me playing the finest tune ever," I said with a twinkle in my eyes, only to find him looking at a girl in a red spaghetti top, red lipstick and red high heels. Too busty. Her blonde hair and green eyes increased her 'vamp' appeal.

"You happen to know her?" I asked cutting short his ogle.

"Oh no, just generally," he said. "So you love CP?"

"Hmm, anyway how come designing?" I asked.

"Haha! A lot of people have been asking me that. It's just that I wanted to be a designer while my parents wanted me to do engineering. So I tried to live up to both. I am currently working with an IT firm, AXZ Technologies. Designing is my hobby that I am planning to take up professionally very soon. I want to make it big. That remains my priority for life," he said.

"Aey! That's sweet. Too ambitious, *haan,*" I said.

"Well let's see, the sweetness does not compare with the sweetness of your voice, umm, I guess we will figure that out later. Your eyes are bewitching my senses," he said and smiled.

"You are just too kind," I said, all cheesy.

"But I am only being mean today," he shot back, twinkling.

I smiled and blushed during our walk, but was not tongue tied. Besides, I did fairly well with the word play, even if he was better. God, I never knew I could be this cool.

✦

We reached there and I ordered a blueberry muffin and a cappuccino and he ordered a latte.

Table No. 11. I remember it. He pulled out a chair and sat himself. For a second, I was rattled, for I thought that was for me but I let it go. I was too much dogged by his cuteness that I ignored quite a lot of things.

"It's okay honey, it's okay," I said to my heart that had been pounding since the moment I saw him, that evening.

"I thought you were taking the chair out for me," I taunted him.

"Oh I am so sorry, I just completely behave like a jerk sometimes," he replied slightly embarrassed.

"Come on! I was just pulling your leg," I smiled.

The order arrived and we were disgusted to spot a fly in his latte. We called the waiter.

"Do you figure out what this is?! We can drag you to the courts for this," I snapped.

"I am sorry ma'am, I'll just get your order replaced," he apologised.

And then entered a paunchy man with receding hairline, the manager.

"Is there any problem madam?" he inquired.

We told him everything. Rishab silently watched me deal with the manager. Don't blame him, when angry, I can make situations so weird for people that they end up getting scared of me.

"Ma'am please calm down. We will serve you a fresh order complimentary. Please give us one more chance," he pleaded.

And this is how I managed a free meal for the two of us.

"W-o-a-h! Temper Lady!" said Rishab, finding his voice at last.

"Yea, somewhat," I said, now shyly.

These were the different sides of me. I could be both angry and shy at once.

"So, how is college going? Do you have any boyfriend?" he asked out of the blue.

We looked at each other and laughed.

"No, umm… I had one long back but things didn't work well, so we broke up," I said.

"Oh! So tell me what went wrong!" he asked.

And he shot me hundred questions or I am exaggerating slightly. But he sounded like an excited school girl.

"How about you? Do you have any?" I asked.

"Boyfriends? NO! I am straight, unlike what people think of designers," he said and winked.

"After that girl-in-red incident, I am more than sure of your orientation. Come on spill the beans now," I insisted.

"Well I have had quite a few GIRLFRIENDS. Eleven, I believe. And I don't shy away from admitting this because I never had that 'she is the ONE' feeling while I dated them. So instead of fooling around with them, I broke up," he said.

"Hmm, so this is your way of finding out 'the ONE'? Going on dating more and even more women?" I asked.

"Yea, you can say that," he shrugged.

"You know I was my ex's first and only girlfriend!"

"Exactly my point, he did not have a history for he had you, and I have a history, for I didn't," he said. And yes, he won the argument again. I was smiling shyly.

The discussions continued. We picked up the car and went to India Gate for a stroll. Seeing us, little beggar kids flocked to us, *"Didi, do rupeya dede, khana khaegi didi, bhagwan tum donno ki jodi banae rakhe"* (Sister, please give two rupees so that we eat food, God bless you couple).

I gave her the chocolate in my bag. She was elated. The torn clothes on her body moved me, indicative of our country's slow path towards development. Rishab also bought her a balloon. She thanked him too, and hopped away.

We started walking towards his car in the parking.

"So we are walking to the end of the parking space?" I asked pulling the most tired face I could.

"I can carry you on my back, if you allow me to," he said flirting yet again.

"I guess, I will do with this *date-turned-evening-jog* thing, for now," I smirked, as we kept walking.

It had started to drizzle and a cold breeze was blowing. He looked at me, and a shiver went down my spine. We were walking and every time our hands touched by mistake, it felt very different and pleasant. It was all very beautiful: the clean wide roads, yellow street lights, lush green trees and the fragrance of wet mud overwhelmed our senses.

We reached the dark and deserted parking lot. On entering the car, our gazes locked. Things moved quickly. I reached for his neck, and his arms automatically dropped to my waist, our tongues played and lips met. He loosened the strings of my *kurti* to kiss my shoulder and neck. His warm breath swooped in on me as I soaked in the addicting vapours of his cologne. The kiss was deep and endless and we did not stop until his phone rang. It was 'Saurabh' who he muttered was a friend. Disconnecting the call, he looked at me with a fresh smile.

"I still cannot believe I have kissed the most beautiful girl I have ever seen."

I returned the smile.

Though I had never imagined this would happen on our very first date, the rain, CP, the warmth of the car and the fragrances had all conspired with the universe for a kiss so perfect to happen.

He kissed my cheek and dropped me home. On reaching my flat and bidding farewell, he kissed my hand again. Reassurance filled our faces, before he drove off. I stood there, watching his car vanish into the darkness of the night.

✦ ✦ ✦

6

When People Fart Smart

I started walking towards the flat, trying to recall the exact sequence of events. I couldn't figure out who had initiated the kiss; it had felt so situational, so impromptu. It was nice. I had kissed a celebrity; just the thought of it gave me a kick. I was happy and dying to tell Niti.

She opened the door drowsily.

"You cannot believe what happened," I gushed.

"Please let me sleep. I have a terrible headache, let's talk in the morning," she said.

"No! This cannot wait; you have to be all ears, RIGHT NOW!!!" I insisted.

She gave me a dirty look and scrambled back into her bed, bundling herself into the blanket. I removed it, shaking her, not letting her sleep.

"Niti please I have to tell you, NOW," I pleaded.

I told her all that had happened between me and Rishab, mind you, every detail. She yawned her way through the conversation until she heard, "We kissed!"

"What? On the first date itself? Desperate people I tell you!" she said, her eyes popping out.

"Shut up, it was all unplanned, like I told you. It wasn't as if we were waiting for this to happen," I resisted.

"Pulling your leg baby! So how was it like kissing THE ENGINEER, DESIGNER and now kisser RISHAB REDDY," she said winking.

"Umm, it was nice and wet," I said blushing, and we burst into laughter, snuggling back into our beds.

I was thinking of Rishab and suddenly a text from him popped up on my screen,"It was a nice evening. And it has still not sunk in that I got to kiss the prettiest girl ever. Have a nice sleep." I slept a happy sleep, all smiles. It was a pleasant feeling.

It was morning; I went upstairs to watch the rising sun again. Believe me, it is the most beautiful sight EVER. The pinkish red sky as the slow golden rays of the sun shone pierced through the clouds, the dew drops on the lilies shining like diamonds, a diadem. Birds that did not cease to chirp. Nature took on her most beautiful form caressing the morning with all her bare charms. I was so moved. The little puppies in the street were going after their mother for morning feed, all of them together. She fed them calmly. Two pigeons were nestled in each other, playing with their beaks; sparrows were picking on the grains at the roof top. Such a blessed sight, a blissful one.

Suddenly, my phone rang and the chain of thoughts interrupted by Rishab's message that read, "Hey, I am at home today, why don't you drop in."

I was a bit hesitant about going to his place so soon after our last encounter. I thought everything was pacing out faster than usual. He lived alone. His parents had been in Bahrain for quite some time now. I thought of talking to Niti, but then dropped the idea. I don't know why.

I went downstairs to find Niti getting ready.

"*Oye*, you leaving so early today?" I asked.

"Yea, have to go for an event at Taj Mansingh today. I will see you in the evening, bye baby," she said and left.

Rishab lived alone and hardly cared about getting his breakfast so I thought I would make some parathas at home and take them along for him in my tiffin box. I had never cooked before but just wanted to give it a try, for him. I was trying very hard this time. These early relationship rituals were fun.

I took a bath and got ready. My light brown *kurti* was all I needed. Kohl-ed my almond-eyes, picked up my phone, texted Niti and left.

I reached Kailash Colony metro station and called him. He did not answer. I tried again, no luck. I stayed at the platform to avoid unnecessary stares from people, waiting for him. After half an hour he answered the call.

"Hey, I am so sorry, had dozed off. I totally forgot you were coming," he spoke drowsily.

"Oh, umm… That's all right. So are you coming to get me from the station," I asked.

"It's a walking distance down my house, just get down and I will guide you."

"Hmm, hmm," I said, mentally taking down directions to his house. I looked at the tiffin in my bag and wondered at the amount of thought that had gone into them, and whether they would elicit the desired response or appreciation. I chose to ignore my sentiments and continued walking.

I spotted him in the balcony of one of the flats as he was speaking to me on the phone still. Quite posh, I could make out. I went upstairs. He opened the door and hugged me tightly. He was tall enough for me to almost dissolve in his huge muscular frame and big long embrace. He was a total gym freak. I went inside and looked around. "The flat is beautifully done," I said.

"You liked it? One of my very good friends has done the interiors for this one," he said.

"Oh, it is beautiful. I love it," I said with a smile.

"Come let's go to my room," he said leading me like his puppet.

And it was one of those rooms you see in the movies. Huge round bed with muslin sheets. A big LCD screen on the wall and an Apple MacBook lying on the bed. Walls were a shade of mauve with some vintage posters framed, hanging on them. The white curtains complimented the room like anything. No, there was no AC, for the house itself was centrally air conditioned. I was swayed off my feet.

I sat down on the bed and switched on the television. NTV it was and some reality show was being aired. It was as dumb as anything could ever get. I begged Rishab to change it but he swore not to change the channel and was drooling over those semi-naked women like anything. I was obviously pissed to see him do that.

I moved away and he only noticed when the show broke for advertisements. *What a jerk,* I thought.

"Awww, I am sorry baby, come here now," he said, arms outstretched for me.

"Oh, so you realised, why don't you go and date one of those," I said, totally expressing my anger.

"I would have, but then none of them has what you do... Those eyes. Those pretty, innocent eyes," he said, making a puppy face.

I smiled and he came closer to hug me. He tweaked my cheek until that show started again. I kept quiet and watched the show, which was actually funny. Such dimwits I tell you. I don't understand what planet they came from or lived on. Once in a while, Rishab would hold me and kiss my cheek. It was cute.

"Are you hungry? Let's order some food!"

"I have got some parathas for us for lunch. I will microwave them if you want," I said and smiled.

"Oh that is so sweet of you Naina, but do you not feel like having a pizza right away? I have this sudden craving for it, you game?" being as different as someone could be.

And a shrug was all the heads up he needed from me, as he went ahead and placed an order at the Domino's. My paratha dreams bit the dust, while pizza took the cake. My heart sank multiple feet.

After the pizzas arrived, and I took a bite or two, only to clean up the mess later, whilst he watched *Dexter* on Star World and gorged on more Domino's. He said, he felt sleepy and asked me to turn off the lights. I felt creepy and nervous, though I did as asked. I went towards the bed and sat down in a corner with a hundred thousand butterflies doing a *cha-cha-cha* in my tummy.

"Why don't you come here in my arms?" he offered with a warm smile. A very pleasant one.

I gave in. I was so hypnotised by his charm that I was doing it all without hesitation. I could feel his warm breath frisking my cheek. We cuddled close and the blanket was over us. The dim lights and mutual intimacy was suggestive of what would or was about to happen. Rishab nudged closer, climbed on top of me and we kissed. I could feel his thick luscious lips and the wetness. The tongue fight continued, I grabbed his hair as his fingers raced down my neck. Before his hands could explore my body further, I pulled away. It felt weird. After a sudden rush of estrogen, I just did not want to do it! I was not ready for it. A voice inside my head negated everything that was happening and I politely listened to it, asserting my will.

"Can we just lie down and sleep in each other's arms?" I asked instead.

"Whatever you are comfortable with, doll," he said and smiled.

We hugged each other and slept for a couple of hours, after which he dropped me home. It was a cute day. But I still felt weird for what had happened in his room. Many such days followed, as Rishab was jobless during those days, for he had recently resigned from the IT firm where he worked. I tried to avoid going over to his place but the scorching sun, hardly left an option. I was just not ready. I needed my own sweet time.

A month passed like that. It was going great. Niti met him once and said she liked him, but avoided talking about him. She perhaps did not like that her space was now someone else's too. I had hardly spent any time with Niti all this while.

Rishab was very moody. He would revert to my messages and call back at his own whim or fancy. One afternoon when we were at Cafe Brown Sugar in Defence Colony, Rishab took a phone call.

After dropping the call, he said excitedly, "Hey! Saurabh has arrived in Delhi."

Saurabh was Rishab's best friend from his engineering days. They were still thick friends. Saurabh had been working in a steel plant in a distant village around Karnataka for a year.

"Oh that's great!" I said with a smile. "So when are you seeing him?"

"Right now, both of us are going to Saket, Select City Walk and he is coming there," he said.

"But Rishab, I look terrible today, why don't you go and meet him. I shall catch up with him some other time."

"Naina, baby, you can never look bad, you are my sexy bitch, come now. Also, both of us have to tell you something important today," he said and like always, I couldn't win an argument with him.

We met Saurabh and sat down in some cafe. He was very funny and both of them would pull my leg every now and then. They were too similar to the extent of sharing the same hobby. Both of them had a way with designing. After a while they finally broke the news to me.

"We are starting out our own business together. A fashion house," they chimed in chorus.

"OK, but you don't have to sound like little school girls. Congratulations boys," I laughed.

They started discussing their plans together and no matter how much they tried to make me feel a part of their conversation, I felt excluded. They told me that they had already had a word with some people in the field and that things were falling in to place.

Well, I was happy for the two of them, but now I was worrying. I did not know what to do after my third year. Mass Communication was on my mind but there was no plan B to fall back on. Discussing so with Rishab would not be appropriate either. He would be so busy with setting up his new business venture. Quickly I texted Kritti to meet up as soon as possible.

Kritti was like my own sister. We were in the same school and then we both came down to Delhi for graduation. Kritti studied B.Sc. Computer Science (hons.) in Shaheed Sukhdev Singh College of Business Studies so she had taken up a PG there. Her parents lived in New York. They had gone there a long time back when she was only 6 years old. She was the only child so they had left a housemaid to attend to her, though, most of her time she spent at my place. We were neighbours. Uncle and Aunty hardly ever made it to Kritti's important days like her school farewell or even birthdays. She addressed my mom and dad as Mom and Dad. She was that close to my family. I knew she missed her parents, but it never showed. Beneath her hard exterior was a childish innocence and simplicity.

I boarded the metro to Rajeev Chowk for Connaught Place, in the evening rush hour. The metro was fairly empty but as soon as the gates opened at Kashmere Gate, I was amazed by a swarm of fat, middle aged aunties playing musical chairs to grab a seat in the already crowded compartment *"thoda sa adjust kar lo beta"* (please adjust a little my son) and you had to abide by it. This was the lucky half. The deprived half would be standing so close to the seat and usually three pairs of eyes glued to grab one seat as soon as anybody got up to leave. And a victorious smile would dance on the face of whoever managed a seat before the others.

I was amused, until strange odours trapped me in their midst. I wanted to rush out of the metro and away from the foul unpleasant fumes of somebody's digestive tracts but the station was far away. Flatulence is the biggest worry that plagues Delhi's public transport, I had read somewhere. Public farters never hesitate to make a move, for they know they will never be tracked down amongst so many people. Oh, how I breathed easy after the doors finally opened at the next station!

It was packed like sardines by now. Not so much in the women's coach. In the general coach, men struggled not to cross the line of control between the two coaches; if they did, the women could, by right, beat them and abuse them in public. The women's coach had only created a divide. Benefits? I did not see any. With such clear demarcation in place, it was now all the more scary to travel in a general coach anymore. They looked at you like you were standing naked.

In twenty minutes, I reached CP and called Kritti. She was waiting for me in B Block's CCD. I went there and hugged her.

"What? What's wrong? So much love?" she asked.

She was always sarcastic, but loved me the most. I knew that. I had always known that.

"Kritti, I just don't know how to carry on with my career. I am too confused. Rishab is going to be busy now and Niti is busy with her internship. You never have time for me," I said in one go.

"Oho, you don't have to worry; things will fall into place, just stay focussed."

We ordered a coffee and a chocolate fantasy and the CCD guy returned. It was a familiar face.

✦ ✦ ✦

7

Of Random Encounters

I stared at him for quite a while and realised he looked like Rishab. I immediately texted him, "Hey, one of the CCD boys looks exactly like you… Miss you already!"

He did not reply. *Must be busy,* I thought.

Kritti got a call from her friend. Meanwhile, I got up from our table to take another look at the CCD boy. I was walking in his direction blindly when suddenly a huge woman with a tray in her hands bumped into me and I almost disappeared within her gigantic breasts. Thankfully, her stomach worked as a cushion which managed to bounced me off and I fell, making a fool of myself. Everyone stared. Embarrassed, I wanted the floor to open up so that I could dig my head and not see their faces peeping in my direction. Kritti, oblivious to what had happened, was still on the phone.

That fat woman did apologise but my anger was eclipsed by the awkwardness and I hardly heard anything. Out of nowhere, a hand came stretching towards me. I held it and got up.

"So, are you OK?" he asked smiling.

That was the warmest of smiles and the most handsome features ever. He carried a very intriguing look that didn't shout for attention but still you could not help but unravel the mystery behind the calm face. Dusky complexion, black eyes, cropped hair and the perfect set of teeth, right from Colgate's advertisement, he wasn't too tall – 5'8" maybe and a lean build.

"Thank you, I am better," I said and smiled.

He handed me some tissues and walked me to my table.

"You seemed lost," he observed.

"Yea, I was actually following that, ehh… Was looking for the washroom," I lied quickly.

"Be careful the next time. Try not to bump into someone that huge," he said, turning to leave with a smile.

"Let me hope you will be there to help me out next time too," I said though, unable to quite figure out why.

He turned and said, "I always will be," and went away.

I went to Kritti, who was still on the phone. We had our share of gossip. She was still oblivious of what had happened. We left after Kritti was done chatting with not me alone but some ten other people over the phone. Kritti and her phone are inseparable. She has to make sure she looks at it every fifth second and keep speaking to everyone possible. Keep talking, is Kritti's byline.

When I reached home, Niti was asleep. I changed and slept, thinking about the encounter with the other CCD guy.

✦

The next day was the last working day for the college before Diwali vacations. I didn't have plans to go home as Niti was staying on for her internship. I had decided to visit there for the Diwali weekend only.

College was almost deserted, it being the last working day. I would always turn up on such days, for something or the other would be pending. This time though, it was something different. Niti and I had problem with our second year mark-sheets. The internal assessment marks were not added which means we were marked zero out of hundred. A lot of university office rounds to various deans, admin officers and even the Vice Chancellor were on the cards. This was a glitch on the part of the university and the college personnel but we students suffered the consequences. On one such round to the university office, I saw a large group of students protesting against the semester system, which was the latest agenda on the changed university guidelines. I don't know what got into my head but I joined them too. I was free anyway as Niti had gone for her first day at internship.

"Veepak Bental Down Down," was the slogan they shouted. Veepak Bental was the then Vice Chancellor. There was a guy beside me who looked familiar, when I peered from the corner of my eyes, not making it too obvious but figuring out it was the CCD guy who I saw last night. I approached him confidently.

"Hi, Naina, Daulat Ram," I said, offering a hand shake.

"HEYYY!" he was still as warm, "Aarian, Khalsa College," he said with a smile.

"So, how did you guys come here, are you a part of some student political body or something?" I asked.

"Well no, I have come here voluntarily. And you?"

"Voluntarily."

We discussed the issue and jelled instantly. He was nice to talk to. Intellectual and sharp. Suddenly a group of students had an argument with the police there and it soon morphed into a fight. More policemen came and started a lathi charge. People ran in several directions. Chaos broke out. Aarian held my hand and we ran too. A policeman was about to hit us but we bent down saving ourselves from a hard blow.

We managed to gallop to a place which was safe and from where we could seize a view of the site. A boy was managing his pyjamas while escaping from the battlefield and a few were bravely fighting their way through the battle. We felt sorry for the predicament of the people and left the place. We went to the Nirulas right opposite the Faculty of Arts.

"It's all sad. There is no tuning between the students' union and the university," I said.

"That is University of Delhi for you," he said and we laughed.

After a round of discussion on ideas and issues, our alma matter came to rest when a clip of Salman Khan dancing to Dabangg's title track screened on live media.

"Oh he was so amazing in the movie," I said.

"You really liked Dabangg?" he asked shocked. The expression on his face was as horrible as if I had said I liked Akon to a Pink Floyd fan.

I asked him, "Do you like Pink Floyd?"

"Like? Phhbbtt! I worship them," he said with a shine in his eyes.

"Great," I said smiling. "And I loved Dabangg! It was so funny, especially the dialogues," I said and giggled.

He looked at me with a cute weird look that conveyed *'you have a sad sense of humour but cute still,'* I simply shrugged and smiled.

After having *Rajma chawal,* both of us bid farewell to each other and left. He was a very decent guy. The ones whom Niti would call *'the Sahil Sarabhai-ish'*. You're guessing it right if you thought about *Sarabhai vs Sarabhai.* We had coined this term for those guys who seemed to have a spine, were decent, intellectual, responsible and adorable. The rarest breed indeed. I smiled, heading back to my flat.

Empty flat, no Niti, nothing to do. Facebook came to my rescue. I logged in and after having seen some new pictures that Rishab had put up recently with hundreds of women and him drooling over them, going gaga, I looked for Aarian Mehra. He was right there in the University of Delhi network. A display picture that best represented him. Him, drinking coffee and looking outside the window. Quite intense, I thought to myself and without delay clicked on *Add as Friend*.

Barely two minutes passed when the notification popped up on my screen, **Aarian Mehra has accepted your friend request, via blackberry.**

Two seconds later, I opened his profile checking out his whereabouts. He was a member of the youth forum 'Leaders for Tomorrow' that I had wanted to join. And now that I was free, I thought I would ask Aarian how to go about it.

✦

It was four in the afternoon and I thought I should probably catch a nap. But the moment I lay down, a swarm of mosquitoes entered my room, buzzing around and biting me by turns. Harassed beyond wits, I picked up the mosquito repellent racket and unleashed an official war against the pests. The one around the fridge, the ones hiding in the curtains, those escaped into the drawing room, my assault weapon spared none. It was an ordeal for an hour and a half and another caught my sight when the doorbell rang. I couldn't let it go, so I jumped from the bed almost like a ninja with my arm outstretched to kill this last bloodsucker and then with a victorious smile, I opened the door. It was Niti, back from her first day at the internship.

"What on earth took you so long to open the door?" she asked. "And why do you grin so much?"

"I was making sure none of those damn mosquitoes remain to bother my baby," I said, giving her an air kiss.

She smiled and entered the house, only to find the drawing room turned into a bedroom and the bedroom, ehh a store room. She shouted at the pitch of her voice "Naina! What the hell have you been up to?!"

"I will put the things in place, calm down please," I said fearing the new sight of her. Yes, the same sight I told you about. The flaring nostrils, her hair appearing to stand midway in air while she went into that mood and her eyes ready to pop out anytime with the violet, green, or whatever lenses they were that she wore and flashed religiously. I hated them.

"Anyway, how was the first day at Ernst and Young?" I asked. And she suddenly seemed to have forgotten the mess around, got talking to me, all excited about the day.

"Oh that's a great place I tell you! Amazing people, free lunch and super hot boys," she said with a twinkle in her eyes.

"I am so jealous," I said making a face and told her about the university incident and Aarian Mehra.

"He seems quite *Sahil Sarabhai-ish,*" she said and I grinned. The moments when your friends realise what exactly you meant.

"I am thinking of joining this youth forum, Leaders For Tomorrow. I am anyway free during the vacations," I told her. "Aarian is also a member there."

"Hmm, sounds good to me. So how is it going with Rishab," she asked. I realised it had been a whole day and there had been no message or call from Rishab and I couldn't contact him either. Thanks to the matter at university, Aarian, and the mosquitoes outrage.

"Err, good," I said hesitatingly and she could guess from my face that there had been no communication since morning.

"Call him now. I will clean the mess," she said and smiled.

Instantly, I dialled his number to get a *call waiting* tone. I thought of calling him later. *Busy man, etcetera.* So I helped Niti tidy up our apartment.

✦ ✦ ✦

8

When I Almost Pulled Off An Action Sequence

The next morning I woke up late. The whole night I had tussled with the pillow, tossing from side to side, trying to sleep. Rishab and his indifferent attitude were getting unbearable. I tried consoling myself that he was busy but the woman on the phone tells me that the phone was switched off.

I diverted my attention to organizing the flat and then after breakfast, settled down before the computer. The usual routine – Gmail–Facebook–Twitter. *Aarian Mehra is now friends with someone* was on my home feeds. I decided to message him right then about joining 'Leaders For Tomorrow' or LFT as it was popularly called.

I wanted to divert my mind from being ignored by Rishab. I messaged:

> *Hey, how are you doing? Well, I figured you are a core team member of LFT, I was willing to join it. Let me know how to go about it. Best, Naina*

I was just looking around his profile and he reverts back almost immediately.

Hey Naina, very well! How have you been? And well nothing much, just a nominal fee and the rest I will tell you. I live nearby only, why don't you just meet up today? There is a meeting too, of the documentary screening committee of which I am a member. If you want to join you are most welcome.

I texted in the affirmative and we agreed to meet up at CCD, Kamla Nagar at 1300 hours.

I got dressed in my favourite green *kurti*. It was a little tight fitting and flaunted all my curves flamboyantly. The silver earrings, a black bindi, the convention of kohl completed and I was ready to leave. There was still time. So I picked up the laptop and wrote a poem: "A tale of their love."

I moved out with my clutch and keys towards the market to the CCD. A black khadi kurta, jeans and kohlapuris, he looked great. Too much like those conventional handsome looking Punjabi boys. I went ahead and he pulled out a chair for me. This guy was quite chivalrous too.

"Hey, you have pretty eyes and Christ they are like a new born's – so cute and big, they are almost popping out to say hi," he said and smiled.

"Thank you and yes, hi!" I smiled, almost blushing.

"So what do you want to have?" he asked.

"Umm… Nothing really, I guess a cappuccino would do."

"Great then, two cappuccinos should be good," he said and went ahead to place the order while I flipped the phone to drop Rishab a text.

Someone held me from behind and before I could get up to see who it was, he came and stood before me. It was Puraan. A junior from school and one of my besties.

"What are you doing here in Delhi?" I asked, hugging him.

"Dad got a transfer so I shifted here in Delhi."

Puraan was three years younger to me but was as smart and mature as any guy of my age would be. He was rather smarter. It was strange but we were great friends. I used to call him my favourite boy, I remembered.

"So what are you doing here, in Kamla Nagar?" I asked.

"My sister is throwing a party tonight, she got placed, so was looking for a gift for her."

Aarian arrived meanwhile and I introduced both of them.

"Naina, you must come to the party. And get your boyfriend along too," Puraan said.

I looked at Aarian, he was smiling. And with a smile I told Puraan that he wasn't my boyfriend and promised him that I shall try. It was difficult to refuse him an invite as he was too dear to me, so I thought I would go along with Rishab perhaps.

A girl and two boys came and greeted me and Aarian. They were from LFT. I bid Puraan goodbye and joined all of them. The meeting was about a documentary screening on food security at the American Center after a week. Aarian, a noted orator, spoke about all that was relevant to the forthcoming event in the meeting. As he spoke, all of us looked up at him in admiration.

The meeting ended an hour later and everyone left.

"So you are leaving for your flat?" he asked.

"Umm, yeah… Got nothing else to do."

"Why don't you join me for lunch?" he asked.

I agreed, and we headed towards the 975 cafe.

I called Rishab during our walk. A couple of more calls to him went unanswered. The tension was building up now and very apparent on my face.

"You look troubled!" Aarian said as we settled at the café.

"Umm, yes there is this guy, we have just started seeing each other and he has not been answering my calls for sometime. I am just worried," I spoke hesitantly.

"Look Naina, there are certain things in life we don't have control on and we must leave them to fate," he said and smiled putting his hand on mine, "If it's meant to be, it will be."

Those words were enlightening, indeed. I felt better and smiled. He was right, if it was meant to be, I needn't worry and if otherwise, I did not really think about it then.

"If I may ask, are you seeing anyone?" I asked.

"No," he said after a brief moment. "I just broke up."

"Oh, I am sorry," I said.

"Don't be, like I said, if it was meant to be, it would have been," he said and smiled again.

It was amazing how effortlessly that smile lightened his face. A face that was melancholic but at the same time promised hope. He was intriguing.

We left for our places after lunch, bidding each other bye. He was a nice guy. It was a pleasant day.

✦

I reached home and in a matter of minutes, Niti arrived too. And then entered Tanya.

"My boyfriend is too possessive, he doesn't even let me go out with my girlfriends, forget the guys. He keeps deleting them from my friends list on Facebook too," said Tanya as she entered.

"Why do you take all his nonsense?" I asked, and a very dramatic reply followed.

"Because I love him."

Niti and I laughed, patting her head.

"Guys, there is a party tonight by one of my friends, at F-Bar, want to come along?" I asked.

Both of them jumped as if they'd been told Hrithik Roshan is posing nude for them. The plan was on. We were going to Puraan's party that night. I took out my red tube dress and black six inches gladiator heels. The pearl bracelet, Kohl, hair loose and done!

Niti slipped on a skimpy spaghetti top and denims while Tanya wore this signature black tube dress she used for every party type occasion. Today was no exception. We called for a cab and reached F-Bar. The music was good, so was the crowd but I could not locate Puraan anywhere. I had even forgotten to take his new number. So we decided to chill for some time before we found him. We had a few drinks and were ready to groove with the music.

"The way people are looking at you, it almost appears to me they are thinking of taking you home," Niti said.

"But it is you alone, my love, who will have the pleasure!" I mocked, as we danced.

We would always do the dirty girl dance together. That night all eyes were on us and I am sure they took us for gays. Tanya was busy drinking and talking to a guy.

After some time, things did not seem as pleasant at her end, so we rushed to the bar.

"Excuse me, this is our friend. We will take care, thank you," Niti told the guy, while he was trying to pull her arm.

"I will take good care baby doll, don't you worry," he said and a gross smell entered our nostrils, while he grinned with his yellow teeth stained with tobacco. He was definitely too drunk. It occurred to me that we were perhaps in the wrong party, for he was shouting at the bouncers like they were his slaves.

"Sir, I guess we are at the wrong party, we must leave," I said.

"Why don't you come along baby, I have men who will take care of you," he said and I was disgusted by that smelly grin on his face.

I did not understand what to do and suddenly he appeared out of nowhere. Aarian. He was dressed pretty well and he, with a conviction in his eyes, kept his hand on the man's shoulder.

"The girls are with me," he said. *Could life be more filmy?* I mused.

Before Aarian could utter another word, that giant almost would have punched him, had I not hit him with a stool. Aarian held my hand, I held Niti's and she held Tanya's and all of us ran to save our lives. Aarian drove us out of the place in his car in no time.

"Thanks for having saved me from that punch," he said.

"Thank you, had you not been here, I don't know what could have happened tonight," I said as Niti tried to console Tanya in the backseat of the car.

"So what were you exactly doing there?" I asked him.

"Stalking you," he teased.

I insisted but he only kept changing the topic; I let it pass.

He not only dropped us at our flat but also helped us to take Tanya to her's. He was very sweet indeed. I wondered how he and Niti would pair up amazingly. They both were so alike.

We thanked him for the hundredth time and bid him farewell.

While we came to our room, I asked Niti, "How do you like him?"

"Oh, he is great, such a perfect guy!" she exclaimed.

"So should I try and hook the two of you up together," I asked her with a shine in my eyes.

"Umm... OK," she said and we shouted and hugged each other, then laughed and slept.

I dialled Rishab's number for the last time. He did not answer. I was worried now. I managed to sleep and thanked God that Niti did not ask about him.

I texted Aarian, a 'thank you' and wished him goodnight.

His reply, "I will let goons bother you if you thanked me ever again."

I smiled and slept. It was an eventful day.

✦ ✦ ✦

9

A Fling?!

It was a lazy Sunday morning. We got up very late. I followed the routine, that is, checked my mobile before anything else. That is exactly how days start, don't they? To my surprise and relief there was a missed call from Rishab. I called him almost immediately.

"Hey, hi," he said.

"Umm... Hi! Where have you been, Rishab? I was worried," I said.

"Hmm, I was a little occupied Naina, you know the whole idea of setting up a new business is too tiring."

"You sound different, is everything all right?"

"Not really, mom-dad aren't too happy with the whole idea of me opening my own fashion house. They don't want me to give up on my privileged career in the IT sector."

"Hmm...! But see, you always knew this, don't feel upset and wait for some time, it will all be great."

"Look Naina, I knew this would happen, but I can do without you telling me this. Please save your lecture for someone else. Bye."

And he slammed the phone. For a minute I was flabbergasted, wondering what was so offensive in what I had said. But then, I reasoned, it was me alone he could vent his anger on.

Saurabh's family is all cool with it as business is considered as good as worship there.

I texted Rishab, "I am sorry honey but I can be ears if you want. Promise, not a word from my end."

He replied, "There is a party at Saurabh's place, be ready at around eight. I will come to pick you up."

That was so abrupt I thought. Anyway I started the very usual fiddling with my wardrobe. While I was trying to take a dress out, the whole of it came falling over me, making a heap. I managed my way out of it and exactly after some one hour forty minutes, I had decided I would wear that short cute black tube dress I had. It had a big bow behind and would show more than it would hide.

I went to the parlour to get all decked up for the night and spent the day doing my hair, polishing my nails, ironing clothes and catching up with some beauty sleep. I slipped into that amazingly short dress, my white legs glistened like snow. I let my hair loose, applied a thick layer of mascara on my kohl-ed eyes, and wore black six inch stilettos, my favourite clutch, Burberry cologne all sprayed and Yippee. Done.

When Niti arrived she stood there watching.

"You send jitters down my body, girl; I am sure Rishab will go weak in the knees today," she said holding my arms.

"Thanks sweety, but I don't know I am not feeling too good about anything these days," I said.

"Naina, just go, get high and have some fun. Also, you smell incredible," she said, and almost in a split second Rishab dropped in. I hugged her and made my move to leave.

"Niti, the wardrobe is all down, please mend it," I said and almost ran in those six inch heels to save my life.

She shouted from behind, "Ahoy! Captain is in a good mood today, the task shall be accomplished only if you promise me to have fun."

I was startled! She was awesome. I kissed her in the air from downstairs and shouted, "I promise to get drunk and get laid today baby I love you," waving her goodbye.

The smile vanished from my face as soon as I met Rishab in his car. We drove towards Saurabh's place. The journey was a quiet one. We had lost conversation. Though he did mention vaguely once that I looked great.

✦

We reached Saurabh's place. It was small and cute. A terrace party housing around ten to fifteen others. On reaching the place, all eyes fell on me. That was indeed an ego kick but then I was feeling awkward now. These women were clad in bare minimal clothing, yes, less than mine, drank profusely and were throwing themselves all over the men. Rishab was dancing with one such woman in no time and I observed the lunatics from a distance. Saurabh came up to me, he was very drunk.

"Hello Madame, may I have the pleasure of dancing with you?"

"Saurabh, you are better off with the woman who was just all over you a moment ago," I advised grinning.

"So you are jealous you couldn't be in her place?" he said nastily.

"You wish!" I said and went on to look for Rishab.

He was nowhere around. I wanted some moments of peace so I decided to detour and look around Saurabh's house. As soon as I reached the stairs, I heard someone calling for Rishab. What I saw there weakened my knees, the ground had slipped below my feet. Rishab was kissing a girl. They were making out with passion. His hands were fiercely coursing down her body and she took him apart by turn. They stood leaning against a wall. I couldn't believe what my eyes had just seen. I raced back to the terrace, to the noise, to forgetfulness. The peace of forgetting was too real to put me through the truth again. I did not want to hear what I heard, see what I saw. I simply retired to the noise and crowd upstairs.

First, it had not sunk in that Rishab was kissing someone else. Then, I fell short of breath. My head spun and everything caused a blur as overpowering images of Rishab and that girl raced through my head and heart, creating a dent, forever.

After about fifteen minutes, I saw Rishab walking towards me. He held me by the waist and advanced closer to kiss me. I moved back, he looked quizzically into my eyes and stopped.

"What's wrong Naina?" He asked.

"Rishab, is there anything you want to tell me?" I asked, my voice breaking up.

"Where does this come from? Please don't ruin the moment, let me just kiss those little pink lips. Why are you always so serious? Just loosen up a bit, babe," he said and made another move. I stopped him again.

"Rishab, I want to know it now," I said rage building up.

"Ok Naina, there is something I have always wanted to say but couldn't gather guts to, I don't want to lie but I don't want you to be on a hook. My mom-dad will never agree for the two of us because of the whole inter-caste thing you know. Moreover, after this whole fashion house business and stuff, things have messed up even more with mom-dad, you know. So it has become all the more difficult. I don't think we have a future together," he said and I gave him a blank look. He had left me by now and was not even facing me.

With tsunamis struggling inside my eyes, I stood there, frozen.

"Naina, I really don't have anything to say. I just want you happy even if it means you start dating someone else to move on. I didn't know how to put this before you but I am glad you asked."

Most of our life is not about what things happen to us but about what choices we make. And then there are the choices that face a consequence. Love or hate. To be a hero or to be a coward. To fight out or to give in. To live or die. And it's not always in our hands. I chose to stay silent. He didn't deserve my words. They, anyway, won't change anything.

I didn't want to tell him that I had seen what he was doing down there and he need not try to bring this caste issue in between, while all he could do was scratch his balls. That I knew he cheated on me. I stood there, waiting for him to tell me the truth. But he didn't. I had lost out on words in those moments. My stomach was shrinking from within and I couldn't breathe.

My legs had become heavy; they felt like I was dragging myself with too much pain. I was being cheated on, all this while and I did not even know! Was this a fling for him?! Was I one of those dumb girls who fell for him, and the ones he dumped with absolutely no regrets? He made me look like a fool. With these and a lot more questions waging a war inside my head, I left Saurabh's house and took an auto home.

The world was spinning around me. I couldn't come to terms with how my life had fallen apart like a castle of cards. All it took him was some fake excuse as to why he should be ditching me and there he lay kissing, holding, touching some other random woman from the party. I felt disgusted even recalling the times those same lips had brushed against mine, the times he had touched me. I was blown away into a pit.

I reached home at around eleven o'clock that night. Rishab called twice or thrice. I had turned my phone off. Niti opened the door and I broke down in her arms. I told her everything about Rishab's version of the story, the ill-suited match, etc. But I still couldn't narrate what I had seen.

She hugged me tightly. I kept sobbing. The kohl had smudged and was no longer there. Nor would it ever be there now.

I was hurt.

You know when you were a little kid and believed in fairy tales? That fantasy of a prince charming carrying you off the hill on a white horse. Yes, the one where he held you and the story ended in a kiss under the stars. Mine had just ended. With a kiss planted on someone else's lips, with my prince charming who wasn't a Shahrukh Khan but a Gulshan Grover. With all this in my head, I kept sobbing.

Niti made sure I was in bed after I changed. She slept and I hugged my pillow, collecting whatever was left of my dreams.

I don't know why, it was all suddenly over. But how could I have just not loved him anymore? That night had changed everything. I felt dejected, angry and foolish, and jolted out of love.

I tried to sleep but couldn't. I needed someone to talk to. I wanted to release the anger and other feelings that were bottling up inside me, making it harder to breathe every second. Niti slept peacefully; I did not want to bother her with my worries. I knew she could help me out. But with all the work she had been doing, I knew she must be tired. Maybe some happy memories of friends could help me out. With all this in mind, I looked for someone online. At three in the night, what could I have expected anyway! As they say, 'only owls, watchmen or lovers are awake in the night.' But the chat showed one person still online. And there she was. Sweet old Kritti.

"Hey, what's up Kritti?" I typed.

"Naina, why are you up so late?" flashed her response on the screen.

"I wasn't feeling good, just thought of speaking to someone," and I sent her the 'sad' emoticon.

Naina, I am coming over. I am bringing my roommate's car, so don't worry," she said and went offline before I could protest.

She could never see me worried or low. If she ever heard I was troubled, she would take every effort to make sure I was okay. So much so, that sometimes I wouldn't even tell her I was low to spare her the trouble.

Exactly thirty minutes later, my bell rang! Kritti could beat the F1 players with her driving skills put to test. I opened the door and there she stood in her pink heart print pyjamas. I hugged her and took her inside.

"Have you been crying, Naina? Your kajal is all smudged and your eyes are red," she inquired.

"No, just that…" and I broke down in tears again.

She got me water and calmed me down. She had got for me a whole bucket of Belgian chocolate ice cream from Giani's. She knew I loved it. I poured it in two bowls and both of us sat by the balcony. I gave her Rishab's 'last ditch' spiel.

"Naina, you know you are the prettiest girl ever. And the guy, who loves you, will love you beyond all odds and will make things fall in place. Rishab probably was never the one. You should be rather glad he told you well in advance," she said. But I did not tell her about Rishab kissing that girl in the skimpiest of clothes. I just didn't have the courage to tell her how blind I had been in falling for a man who openly lusted after other women with as much gusto, if not more.

"Kritti, I had started seeing a future with him," I sobbed instead, helping myself to every bit of much needed ice-cream.

"Naina, he has something else in mind. You cannot blame him; he has been like that right? Why even expect something from such a person? I am sure he must be feeling bad too for breaking such a wonderful girl's heart. Believe me, he is the loser here," and she hugged me.

I so adored her. Some relations are so sweet and so pure. Such was ours. We were friends for life. She left at around four in the morning, for she had to take the car back. The moment she left, tears started rolling back down my cheeks.

Rishab and I probably did not spend much time together, but when it comes to relationships, it is the intent, the dreams, that build everything. Intent to trust, intent to love, intent to stay together. And now how everything came crashing down. For him, I was just another girl in the pew, but for me, he was someone who I thought would help me love again. Our relationship had just shattered like pieces of glass before me, proving yet again, that love wasn't to stay in my court for very long. Reality has a way of sneaking up on us and biting us in the ass when we least expect it.

✦ ✦ ✦

10

When The Kohl Goes Missing

The next morning, I did not leave my bed. Niti insisted to stay back from her office that day but I asked her to leave, ensuring I will be good.

"Naina, please don't do anything nasty and better not cry. I will try and come back early," she left, kissing my forehead.

I sat there, in my bed, gazing at the wall like a fool. I hadn't brushed my teeth nor did I wash my face, though I went to the kitchen to get some food for myself. This was intrinsic to me. Depressed or happy, food was something that I always needed. I gorged on some toast and then a bowl full of ice cream, full of Hershey's chocolate syrup. My iPod played 'Wish you were here' by Pink Floyd and I cried. I cried silently. Why did it have to happen to me? I went and sat by the window pane and it had started drizzling. It seemed as if nature was crying along with me and I felt shrinking from within.

I realised with the passage of time that Rishab's episode could have been necessary to free the lover in me, to let go of my apprehensions. Destiny was preparing the lover in me for the love story that was still being written somewhere. The one with a happy ending, the one with a 'forever'. Still I felt ashamed at judging someone so wrongly for the first time ever.

✦

It had been three weeks since and I was convincing myself that I was better. But I was in pain. So much, that it blocked out everything else. When we are troubled, our pain takes centre stage. Pain. We ride it, embrace it, ignore it… And for some of us, the best way to manage pain is to just push oneself through it. For the first few days, I had kept aloof from everything, only to make an important realisation. If love was to come my way, it would find its own course!

My reasoning gave way to the lover in me who was sulking over something not meant to be. And maybe it was for the better. I could not have continued with all the mourning for someone who cheated on me so shamelessly. I never spoke about it to anyone. I couldn't.

✦

Niti had started seeing a guy in her office and was happy. I couldn't hook her up with Aarian because the whole Rishab fiasco had left me drained. Niti and Aarian had become good friends though. They even went to watch a couple of movies together. I never joined them. I was in the 'mourning period' that usually follows a break up.

One day when I asked Niti why things were not progressing between Aarian and her, especially since they spent a great deal of quality time together, she replied vaguely. "Yea he is awesome, but he is too awesome for me. Moreover, he isn't available."

"Excuse me?! What does that even mean?" I asked, baffled but she changed the topic.

I did not revisit the topic because I had stopped talking about love and relationships ever since....

That very day, Aarian called to inform me that there was a meeting in CCD about the film screening which was scheduled for the weekend. I had already missed one in my rough break-up patch. Missing another one, was out of the question.

I reached CCD and saw Aarian reading a book. White shirt and blue jeans, he had pulled it off really well. When did he not look good, anyway? I was sure he looked great even in the lousiest of clothes and on the worst hair days.

"Hey," I greeted him.

"Hi Naina, how are you now?" He knew about me and Rishab.

"I am okay, Aarian. Thanks," I was timid.

As soon as everybody arrived, the meeting took off and Aarian and I were kept in the same team for the coming screening. I was happy about it. I could now work more comfortably. We were five people managing the whole screening.

"So, Naina, you and Aarian can start discussing how to draw the audience and promotions," suggested Ankita, the team leader.

I don't know why but it always occurred to me that she did not really like me. Maybe she had the hots for Aarian and wanted to work with him, but being the team head, she was only supposed to supervise the whole thing. Because Aarian and I lived in nearby premises, it became mandatory for her to assign us the same task. Or maybe, I was, as always, over thinking it.

"Ankita, I am not feeling too well today, can we start this from tomorrow?" I asked.

"See Naina, you have already been too laid-back about the last screening. I will appreciate if you could handle this one responsibly," she said haughtily, leaving with the other two guys.

Everything about her signalled BITCH ALERT!

Aarian and I were sitting. He placed his hand over mine and said, "Don't feel bad. She is only a little strict and tensed about this one. Really nice otherwise."

Why in the world was he defending her rude behaviour? Did he have the hots for this bitch of a woman too? Maybe that is what Niti meant by when she said he isn't available. Stop racing your mind Naina, I told myself. I couldn't have judged her on that bit of a conversation.

"So where do we start from?" I asked Aarian.

"You go home, take rest and I will manage today's work. And don't worry; Ankita will know what she needs to know. Just remember, you worked and that's about it," he winked with a smile.

He was such a sweetheart, I thought. Such kindness. With a wide smile back, I thanked him. The moment I made a move to leave, he called after me, "Naina, though you look great in specs as well, but I am missing those dark kohl-ed eyes today."

"Kohl is back by tomorrow. My word," I said and smiled back.

I could see a great friend in him. He is one of those rare guys you would never feel awkward around. A friend who would understand you, chivalrous, cute and a fairy tale kind of perfect guy.

I felt much better. It was always great being around good people. I reached halfway to my flat when I messaged him, "Hey, I was wondering if you want to drop by my flat, we can work together there."

"Oh, whatever you are good with. Guide me the way, I will be there," he texted back.

I told him the way and headed towards my flat. Isha was waiting outside for me when I reached home. I took her in. She had been worried about my absurd absence, and had come to inquire after me. I told her everything.

"I am good now, Isha. Don't worry. Really," I said.

"*Di*, couldn't you just call me and talk about it?"

"You know I just need to restore myself alone when all down."

"You cannot just not speak about it and seclude yourself, I get worried *Di*."

I was so awed. She has always been so well-disposed to me. She had respected me and loved me like a sister. I loved her too.

Our conversation was interrupted by the doorbell. It was Aarian. I introduced both of them. Isha developed an instant liking towards him! We talked for a while when Isha asked,"*Di*, can you get us something to eat please? Be a nice host."

"Well, I doubt if there is anything at home, but Maggi must be there, I shall get it."

"People have always appreciated my culinary skills and they say I am a master chef with Maggi and coffee," offered Aarian playfully.

"Oh so I will let you, Sir Aarian 'Chef' Mehra, to bestow my kitchen with your steps and bless our taste buds with your specialties," I shot back.

I can bet you, never in my life had I tasted such delicious Maggi or coffee. Although there is nothing you could possibly do to Maggi, this guy changed my stand. He was brilliant.

Isha left after the meal to let us continue working, but I could see that she had enjoyed her time with us. I bid her bye and then saw Aarian reading something. He was reading my blog bookmarked on my laptop. My poems.

"Oh my god, these are wonderful. You write brilliant stuff Naina. Why don't you take up this whole writing business seriously?" he asked.

"Oh come on, you are only being kind. Moreover, I just do it when I cannot speak my heart out to anybody," I said and shrugged.

He looked me directly in the eye and said, "Consider my word. You can really write, give it a shot."

I don't know, I had never thought about it but then something made me say, "I shall try," almost involuntarily. As I heard myself agree, I was stunned. I had never felt so confident, or happy. I was elated.

✦ ✦ ✦

11

That Bitch

I had started seeing less of Niti, she would remain busy with her boyfriend, Sankalp, she told me. She had even started losing some kilos. She was getting paler by the day. I told her not to confine herself to such a strict boiled diet, but she was going absolutely crazy. She had even started taking protein supplements. She was going bonkers over this new guy.

"You are pretty Niti, you don't have to lose weight for someone," I said and smiled.

"Naina, I am doing it for myself. I want to look good," she replied with a straight face.

Strangely, she never introduced me to Sankalp and had also, started behaving unusually. I often asked her to fix a meeting with him but her answer was always the same."He remains busy, Naina. But I will try," and then she would change the topic.

It was as if she deliberated it all. I did not feel good about it. Perhaps she was unhappy because I didn't talk to her much when I was getting over Rishab.

The last film screening was an absolute hit. Ankita had never seen such an audience turnover for a documentary screening ever. She was happy with mine and Aarian's effort. The main event was yet to come, 'The Leaders for Tomorrow Youth Summit' in Mumbai. The task assigned to our team was to manage the fashion show in order to draw funds for the event.

I thought I would ask my college's fashion team 'Debonair' to help us draw funds. I had a word with the team head, Priyanka and things got moving. These girls were awesome. They would set the ramp on fire, I was sure. My team was happy with the progress.

Aarian and I had started to hang out more often than usual. We were great friends by then. I hardly felt the need for anybody when with him. There was a presentation that I had to make for the whole event concerning the functioning, itinerary and arrangements for an upcoming meeting with the chairpersons, trustees and delegates. Though this was Ankita's task, the bitch did not rest until she managed to overload me with work. She was a creep. I hated her.

I was sitting in the very same CCD with Aarian one fine evening, discussing the presentation when the waiter approached our table.

"Mr. Rishab, your credit card isn't working sir," he said as I went numb.

"This is for our table," a group of college students called out to him.

In a split second I was back in the dumps. I became quiet. It was like all my efforts of shunning Rishab-thoughts from my head, and life were only amplifying the pain. And that too without warning.

"So you have been fostering the Juliet ever since the break up?" Aarian asked intuitively.

"Whatever," I said and shrugged.

"Naina, that guy did not even care to call you once and ask if you were ok and you are just not ready to stop behaving like lovesick girls sobbing over their boyfriends," he said irritated.

"I am ok, Mehra," I said, looking away.

"I have a name! Why are you calling me Mehra these days? And anyway, look at me when I am talking to you, we have given you enough time alone, enough things to keep yourself occupied and now you better not sulk anymore. I cannot see my bestie like that," he said with his voice breaking out.

I looked at him and he wore his epic warm, comforting smile. I hugged him.

"Did you just call me your bestie?! Awwww!" I said grinning.

"Oh don't aww me," he said irritated.

"Anyway, you think I will be able to perform this presentation before all the trustees and members in the meeting?" I asked, nervously.

"What do you think I will say?" he asked back, a look of warm assurance on his face.

I smiled. I felt confident when he was around. He was such a morale booster. We paid the bill and walked down the road. University of Delhi's North Campus is one of the most beautiful places to be at in the evenings, whether in rains or winters. The dense greens on the banks of the street, the yellow street lights and students sitting or walking along footpaths, a serenity that could not be confined to words, filled the air.

He dropped me home with the words, "Naina, you will be awesome tomorrow, don't worry."

He must have noticed the frown on my face, I thought. But he never left me with anything but smiles. Niti was not at home. Must be with Sankalp I assumed and returned to work on my presentation. I was done in no time. I just had to add some last minute slides. The doorbell rang, it was Ankita. What the hell was she doing here?!

"Hi, I was just walking around here so I thought, I could just confirm whether you were through with the presentation," she said. "May I come in?"

"Oh yes," I said and let her in.

"Cute flat, you live here alone?"

"No, my flatmate is out with her boyfriend."

"Oh, so can I see the presentation once?" she asked.

I nodded and proudly handed over my laptop to her. I had done it really well, I knew.

In your face, biatch, I said in my mind.

"Can I have some water, Naina?" she asked.

I got her a glass of water as she read through the presentation. Her face revealed that she was fairly pleased.

"That's a really nice one, I must say," she said. "Seems like your week's hard work will prove its mettle tomorrow."

I thanked her and turned the laptop off. She left with her wicked smile.

I was relieved at having completed the presentation. There was a 'Leaders for Tomorrow' party that night and I had thought I would not be able to attend it because of the presentation but now I could make it! I picked up my phone and called up Aarian.

"Hey! Pick me up from home. I am coming to the party; through with the presentation already."

"Oh that's great! It's a late night party so I will drop in at your place around eight to pick you up," he said.

There were two hours to eight and I was all geared up. It would be fun, I thought. I opened my wardrobe and picked up the blue backless halter dress and my favourite golden earrings. Kohl was back. My big eyes, with a tinge of brown and lots of kohl complimented my little pink lips just rightly. I had started getting back to life. I picked up the golden stilettos and was ready half an hour before time.

✦

Niti was reading in her room while I was getting ready. The distance between us had stretched to an extent that we would hardly even know we were in the same house at times. She came home some time back and did not even bother with a hi. This whole cold war was uncalled for and I tried to talk to her many times but she would just walk away pretending there is nothing and that she was just too fatigued with work.

I went to her room and saw her sobbing silently over the phone. I was taken aback. I rushed towards her.

"What's wrong Niti? Why are you crying?" I asked. "And who are you talking to?"

"Nothing," and she disconnected the phone with an effort to control herself.

"Please tell me Niti, I am worried."

"Was talking to Mom, just missing her. Couldn't make it home this Diwali so everyone is missing me there,"she said.

"Awww!" I wiped her tears and hugged her. "You want to come to the party with me?" I asked her. "You have lost so much weight, let's eat something full of fat and cream today, enough of boiled food for you."

"No, I have some office work to do, you go and have fun. Don't worry about me," she said.

"Niti, I am not leaving you like this," I said.

"Naina please go! I am good and I've really got to work. Moreover, I am sure of what shape your wardrobe will be in today. I will mend that too,"she said making a face. Yes, the face I had been dying to see from every time I made a mess of things around.

I giggled and hugged her, preparing to leave for the party. Aarian had messaged that he had almost reached. I went to the door and she shouted, "Naina! I love you."

My woman was back. It was an enthralling day. I was all the more happy. I kissed her and left. Aarian was waiting outside. He saw me and stood there awestruck.

"I need you to pick my jaw up from the ground, please," he said as he stood there with an open mouth.

"Oh shut up, Mehra!" I blushed.

"Naina, you're looking very pretty and it's more because you are wearing something that has been missing for quite a while," he said.

"What?" I asked, confused.

"This smile," he said and I blushed again.

I indeed wore my best smile that day. I was really very happy. I told him everything on the way to the club and he was happy too.

✦

We reached the club and everything was so perfect about the place. The lights, the music, the people. Ankita caught us staring at people and walked up to us. She was a bit tipsy.

"Hey Naina, you look nice. Where did you get this dress from? Sarojini? A fake Mango if I am guessing it right?" she said with that wicked smile of hers.

Aarian held my hand, for he knew I would have punched the woman in her face and butted in, "Though she still manages to get all the eyes hooked on her, including yours. Isn't that great?!"

It was as if someone had told her that we knew she wore padded bras on a flat chest. She stood there open mouthed and I looked at Aarian with surprise. I noticed he spoke only when it was absolutely necessary. He was a man of few but significant words.

My night was made. I danced my heart out on the floor. Aarian was looking at me from the bar. He did not drink. Yes, he did not even drink! Can you beat that? There wasn't one flaw I could find in that guy.

"Come now Mehra, you have to dance," I asked him, tipsy.

"Naina, I am enjoying the best sight from here, you go and dance," he said.

Ankita came up to us. She was drunk. She managed to stand before she threw herself on Aarian. I didn't know how exactly she managed to do that, for I was standing closer to her than he was! What a bitch, I thought.

"I never thought you would come here tonight, Naina," she uttered. Soaked in alcohol, she stank.

"Why do you say so?" I asked.

"Why do you always come and stand between me and Aarian? It was all going great till you came in. I hate you Naina," she said.

It was all clear to me now. She had the hots for Aarian and Aarian's friendship with me bothered her, I could see.

"You are too drunk Ankita, I guess we should talk tomorrow," I said, feeling awkward.

"You will not be there to see any of us tomorrow, Naina. They will throw you out of the forum without the presentation," she laughed.

"What do you mean?" I asked puzzled.

"I mean, I deleted the presentation when I came by your place today and thought that way I will be able to keep you from coming to this party… But you are awesome, sweety. You came and now with no presentation you will be out forever! I hate you Naina! I hate you," she said and passed out.

I was in tears. Aarian was shocked by her malice and ill will. He held me tight and told me not to worry. We left the party that very moment and headed for my place, where Niti was asleep.

"I don't know what I am going to do. I am so screwed Mehra," I sobbed.

"Get your laptop out Naina, please don't panic. I am here, and I will stay here till we figure it out. Please don't worry. It's just twelve right now, we have the whole night to fix this."

I got my laptop and changed into my spaghetti and pink boxers. The presentation wasn't there. I started crying all over again.

Aarian shouted, "Naina, just shut up and go freshen up, I will figure out meanwhile where to start from."

I obeyed and then sat down quietly beside him. I went to the kitchen to get coffee for both of us. We worked our way tirelessly through the night. At least that is what I like to believe. Though as a matter of fact, somewhere in the middle I had dozed off. When? I had no clue.

✦

I got up. It was eight in the morning. Niti was getting ready.

"Niti, was Mehra around when you got up?" I asked her.

"No, why will he be here? How was the party last night, anyway?" she asked.

He must have left early, I thought. I checked my laptop. It was on the sleep mode and on the word document there was a special note:

You looked like a 5 year old cute little girl while asleep. Didn't want to wake you up, so left. The presentation is there in the documents folder. Have a look at it once. Love, Mehra.

I was moved. He was such a kind friend. I opened the presentation and it was awesome. Even better than the one I had made. He was brilliant. Had he not been there, I wouldn't have been able to maintain my place any longer in LFT. I was happy and texted him a 'thank you' message.

"See me there and together we will see Ankita's reaction," he texted back promptly.

Yes, this would make my day now. The presentation was awesome, I knew. All I wanted to see was a surprised, no, shocked her. I wanted to make this the worst surprise of her life. I was ready.

✦ ✦ ✦

12

Realisation #1 And The Kids

I was well prepared for the presentation. I had already run the whole presentation several times in my head and also planned out my ensemble. I was set. I took a shower and got ready as quickly as possible. A beige slim fit skirt with a slit and a crispy white cotton shirt with my white stilettos made for perfect formals. I straightened my hair for a neat look, applied kohl and wore my specs. I checked myself out for one last time in the mirror and was satisfied: yes, I carried it all well.

I called Aarian.

"Hey, thanks!" I said, as he answered the phone.

"It was all your hard work, I only helped a bit," he said.

"My hard work? Yes, sleeping is indeed a lot of hard work, phew," I said, sarcastically.

"Oh come on now, don't be so hard on yourself. I am sure it must have taken some good deal to look that cute while sleeping," he said.

He always left me speechless, and now blushing.

"Tell me where do I see you, I am ready," I said smiling into the phone.

"Oh, too punctual?! Nice! I will pick you up from your flat. I was ready too, so will just leave."

"But Mehra, why are you coming down, it's a matter of five minutes I will come," I wondered aloud.

"Naina, you must be all dressed up, why invite nasty stares. Moreover the heels and the rickshaw don't go really well. So stay there, I am coming," he insisted and then disconnected the call.

I smiled, rushing downstairs to pick up my laptop bag, ready to be received by him.

He looked spectacular. A light pink, striped shirt tucked in grey trousers. He carried formals like those very few men who you come across in the corporates. And standing next to a long white Accord. Phew! A sight worth dying for.

I went up to him and patted his shoulder from behind while he disconnected another call he was on. He hugged me almost immediately. For longer than usual. He looked thrilled.

"So, what is the reason behind this sudden outburst of happiness?" I asked.

"I had sent an application to the New York State University for admission to their film and television programme. I always wanted to do this. Only now, I got their call, they have approved my application!"

"Oh my God, that is so amazing! Congratulations!!!" I hugged him again and was delighted.

"You have so nailed it Mehra! I am so happy," I said, hugging him.

"I know, I know, I will be leaving for New York, imagine," he said.

And suddenly both of us left each other's grip and looked into each other's eyes. Words did not help. There was silence. The sinking feeling that both of us were going to be miles apart. We had become quite used to each other by now.

"Umm, let's leave or we will be late and Ankita will leave no opportunity to take a dig at you," he said, breaking the silence.

"Hmm, let's go," I said and we drove off.

Isn't it funny, we, the grown ups, find ourselves groping for words to express our feelings for each other!

✦

The journey in the car was a quiet one. Something had happened in those few minutes. Something we had been trying to ignore. We were now too dependent on each other. The essentials for life.

"When do you leave?" I asked.

"Immediately after the university exams," he said. "There is just one essay that I have to send them and I will be accepted. I have been working on that essay since the past one year so I am more than sure I will make it."

"Oh, that sounds great," I said.

We reached the summit venue and got down. A hall was booked in this big hotel for the summit. Ankita was nowhere to be seen. Someone said that she was so drunk last night that she couldn't make it to the event. Ankita was thrown out of the team and Aarian was the new head now. I was happy.

My presentation was about to start. I entered the hall full of delegates, media and LFT trustees and members. Initially, I was nervous, but Aarian was right there, standing near the curtains. His presence made me feel at ease.

The presentation was a hit. I saw people nodding in appreciation. My eyes searched for Aarian. I did not see him where he had been standing. I just wanted to run up to him and tell him how thankful I was and how blessed I was to have a friend like him. If it was not for him, I would have given up, I am sure.

I left the stage and looked for him. I saw him coming from a distance. I hugged him.

"So, I see someone just made it big, eh?" he said and smiled.

"It wouldn't have been possible without you," I said.

"Oh please stop praising and thanking me now, please," he said.

"So you better accept, you are awesome."

"I am awesome-est Naina," he winked at me.

We laughed and headed towards the car. We were done with our bits at the event. So we thought we would just leave and spend some time at home with Niti, it was her last day at the internship and moreover the month's break had ended. It was college from tomorrow.

As I looked back, I realised, so much had happened in this one month. I got hooked and broke up. I made one friend for life. Niti started dating someone, someone I never got to meet. My friendship with Kritti and Isha strengthened. In all, it was one hell of a month.

I was lost in my thoughts while Aarian drove me home. We reached Bungalow Road. It would always remain jammed.

I was sitting in the car gazing outside. I had always loved campus and Kamla Nagar and was a little sad that I would soon be leaving it all behind. Bungalow Road was always beautiful and full of life. Freshers, seniors, everyone was equal here. All colours of life were at play. I will miss it. Miss it badly.

But amongst all this that was colourful there, one could see some darker hues. There were cries not loud enough to reach the ears of anyone, I am talking about the beggars who would stand outside the Subway and the Domino's to pick up whatever little were left over in the bin and eat. Yes, from the bin. I saw one such little boy, in rags, picking up from the bin and eating.

"Mehra, you just park the car somewhere and come back here. I will be inside Domino's," I said and left the car before he could say anything.

I went towards that little chap.

"Ahem ahem, someone seems hungry here," I said.

He did not answer.

"Even I am hungry, but have no company for lunch. Would you have food with me?"

He walked up to me and said, "Didi, can I get my sister along as well. She is hungry too. She is small, so she won't eat much."

I was floored by his innocence. The deprivation in his eyes moved me. I asked him to get her.

I took both of them with me to Domino's. The guard stopped them at the door.

"They are with me," I said. But he was adamant. I went up to the manager and talked to him. Those little ones were standing in a corner. Much aware that they weren't a part of the same world. They only kept gazing at the ground. I was all the more sure I had to do this today.

"Sorry ma'am, but we cannot entertain them. Our customers will be uncomfortable," said the manager.

A group of girls who were sitting right next to where I stood probably overheard what was going on. One of them stood up and came to us.

"See, we have no problems and I am sure no one else will do. And for the sake of humanity, can you please let her do what we all should?" she instructed the manager.

He looked ashamed, then let me and the kids in. Everybody in there cheered those little kids who smiled at the attention. Such a naive and pure smile that was! Aarian arrived. He saw me sitting with them and understood everything. He walked up to us and asked, "So can I join you?"

"Didi, is he your *brufin* (boyfriend)," the little girl said and smiled.

Aarian and I laughed and told her we were best friends. We asked their names. The boy was Salman and the girl, Shabana.

"Oh, you have beautiful names. Whom do you live with?" I asked, while Aarian got the pizzas, coke and choco lava cakes for us.

They began gorging on the meal when Salman replied, "We live here with our uncle. Our parents died working in a chemical factory. Uncle takes care of us. He is a rickshaw puller. We help at home by picking up rags in the morning and sell chocolates here during the day."

"Do you go to the school?" I asked.

"There is hardly any money to source food didi, how can we go to school. But my friend Naved goes. His father is a butcher. I try to read his books sometimes. There are beautiful pictures in his books. I like them," said Salman.

Shabana was looking at us and was eating. He said she was only five. Salman was ten.

Tears filled my eyes. Aarian held my hand and I looked at them. My eyes were full of questions. Questions to the universe for being so unfair and partial. While kids of their age go to school and play with toys, these little angels scorch their bodies in the heat and spend their childhood in rags. And while we cry over broken hearts and exams, their cries over an empty stomach are ignored and go unheard because our lives are too busy for them. It was a shallow world, I thought. We all were shallow.

They finished their food and we got up to leave. Shabana spoke up: "Didi, Thank you," she said, tugging at my hands downwards and asked me to bend. She kissed my cheek. I picked her up and kissed her. She was a little princess. Everybody in there had smiles on their faces. For these two kids, for humanity. I looked at Aarian and he whispered those words from a distance, "I am so proud of you."

I paid for all the chocolates Salman was left with and gave them to him. He was happy; he could now go and play with his friends for the rest of the day.

We bid them bye and left for the car.

"Mehra, how much was the bill? And please tell me I WANT to pay for it!" I asked as we got seated.

"Nothing," he said.

"Mehra, please! Tell me now," I insisted.

"Naina, the manager felt sorry for his behaviour and said the food was a treat from Domino's to the kids. He was moved by your stand and realised it was his duty too as a fellow human being," he said and smiled.

I had a big smile on my face. A smile of contentment.

✦ ✦ ✦

13

Of Letters And Parties

Aarian dropped me home. It was five. There were still two hours for Niti to return.

"Let's decorate the house and get food to eat. We will throw Niti a party. She will be happy. Moreover, it was such a great day, we must celebrate," he said.

"Oh yes, that's a great idea. Let's get chocolate truffle cake as well and I will call Isha and Kritti too. I want you to meet Kritti," I added.

"Great then, all the pretty girls and me! May the Goddess of Sweet Love empower me with the Girl-magnet charm," he said.

"As if, this is something new for you, pervert," I said with a raised brow.

"Ya, I have been lucky, you see. I have you, after all, and once we get married we will have kids with pretty eyes, more awesome," he said and nudged me.

"Yuck! You?! Never, eeww… Go!" I shrieked and pushed him away.

He was such a jerk, but a cute one.

Aarian always believed that one should gain as much knowledge from as many sources around. He wasn't a nerd but a knowledge freak. He would sit before the internet and jump from one Wiki page to another before anything caught his interest. This craving for knowledge had led him to enroll in a certificate course at Miranda House, an all girls' college. Miranda was the only college that offered that course and Aarian was able to enroll in it because it was open to boys, but few knew about it. In fact, he made such a brilliant presentation on completion of the course, that the professors even urged him to continue his Ph.D from Miranda if he ever wanted to! Needless to say, he had become the eye candy of a class full of girls! His best friends were all women except for Vinay, who I would always refer to as his gay partner. They at least behaved like that. I would tease them but they were unperturbed. Vinay's girlfriend Uttara was super irritated by their mushy love too.

"OK baby, I am going to get the food, you mend the house," he said, winked and drove.

"Don't you call me baby, you jerk," I protested.

I headed back to the flat and called Isha and Kritti, asking them to reach as soon as possible. There was a letter for me lying on the table. It was from Mom. But why would she write a letter? I went inside, drank some water and opened it. It read:

Naina,

We have finalised your brother's engagement. The girl is Bhardwaj uncle's daughter, Priya. You know her don't you? The engagement is scheduled for next week as Priya has to go out for six months after that, for her office work. I have sent you the tickets for tomorrow along with this letter; call me once you find it. I wanted to call you and tell, but matters like these have to be penned down, you know that right?! Anyway, I have sent Kritti's ticket too. Ask her to come. There are a lot of preparations to be done.

Love,
Mom

Like I said, whenever there was something out of line, letters were the medium of interaction in our family. Actually, these hopelessly romantic genes come from my Dad. He would even now, write chits to Mom and cajole her when she got angry. With utmost enthusiasm, he would recount to us, stories of their courtship, while Mom would pretend not to remember. Though, on one such occasion, I caught her smiling, outside the room, eavesdropping, while Dad told us about their sneak outs, secret dates and romantic encounters. They were the sweetest couple, ever. I loved them.

I called Mom immediately.

"Yo Mommy! Got the letter and the tickets. I am sure *Bhaiya* must be so happy, he always thought of Priya as an amazing girl. I have called Kritti at home today, will inform her then. All good at home?"

"Yes *beta*, all is good. Call me once you board the train, okay?

"Mumma, I will call you in a while. I guess there is some problem in the network. Bye Mom!" I said and kept the phone down. I had to blame the network connection for not having to listen to her reminder on my daily quota of milk, the drink I hated most.

There was another letter on the table, from Niti. This was strange. It read:

Naina,

I have left for home. I am sorry something urgent has cropped up. Don't call or try to reach me, I will be fine. Tried calling you but couldn't reach.

Miss you.

Love,
Niti

What was this now? How could she just leave like that? What was she even thinking? What was wrong with her? Why the hell was she ignoring me so much? All these questions festered in my head. We had just cleared the misunderstanding the day she was sobbing in her room. Maybe she thought she wasn't as close to me as Aarian was now. She gets insecure at times and this could be one such instance. But there was no one who could possibly answer me. I sat looking at the letter and thought where did I go wrong and had no answers. The doorbell rang.

"You haven't even started with anything Naina?" Aarian asked as I opened the door.

"Oh what's wrong? In a pensive mood all of a sudden?" he asked.

"Niti has left for her home. She left this letter for me," I said giving him the letter. He read it.

"Naina, don't think too much. There must be something. Let her get back to you, okay?" he said.

"There is another letter from Mom," I said handing him the other letter.

"Oh boy! You guys write letters to each other. That is sweet!" he said and smiled.

Was he serious or sarcastic? Another Rajeev Shergil (my father) here? I thought, while he was reading it.

"Many many congratulations, Naina! This is such good news! See, we have a reason to party anyway!"

"Yeah, though I am scared. I know what will happen there. All the old fat aunties will come up to Mom and say, *Ohh! Naina has turned so pretty. Now she is about to graduate as well. It's her turn next* and they will pull my cheeks apart," I replied, frowning.

I hated this. I had always avoided appearing in functions because of this. These aunties appeared to be more worried about you. When you studied, they were more worried about what level college you got into. If you were a girl, as soon as you were about to wind up graduation, they would worry about your marriage. After you got married, they were worried about whether you had kids or not. Sometimes, I wondered whether my Mom and Dad worried as much as these relatives did. This always got on my nerves.

"Hahahahaha!" Aarian laughed. "It is typical of you, Naina. But you are mistaken, they will never say, Naina has turned so pretty."

"Shut up, you jerk. You are so mean," I said and turned away. And the bell rang again.

Both of them had arrived, Kritti and Isha. I described the plans repeatedly and Kritti was elated. She loved family functions, maybe because she hardly saw any, except for the ones at my place.

I introduced Kritti and Aarian to each other. Although Kritti hardly ever talked to new people, they gelled well in no time. Now that all my friends were around, I missed Niti even more. I had planned all this for her, after all.

We had a fairly nice time that day. Cake, food, music, liquor and what more did one need than the company of best friends? I was happy. I had all the reasons. But Niti's absence kept bothering me.

✦

I began packing for the next day. The moment I opened my wardrobe, a smile crept up my face. My bitch had mended it again before leaving. Now I understood why Mom's letter was open in the first place. Niti must have read it. She must have done my wardrobe so that I would be able to find my clothes with ease. She was such a sweetheart. I missed her all the more. How I wished her closer.

I called up our class representative at the college and informed her that Niti and I would not make it to college the next week.

I packed everything and slept. It was weird, sleeping without Niti. Not that we shared a bed but the very aura of her presence was homely and warming. Why did she have to go like this? I kept wondering and slept.

✦ ✦ ✦

14

Of Railway Station And Of Clichés

It was a pleasant morning. I was going home. But I knew what my homecoming would be like. Mom would stuff me with all possible varieties of parathas and not to mention the dreadful, milk! And to tell you about her parathas, they were literally as thick as that maths book we used to study in school. There would be layers of ghee over them. She wouldn't rest until she made me eat those. Typical of moms! Paranoid about our eating habits!

I called Kritti. We were to meet at the New Delhi railway station at three. It was eleven o'clock. I checked my phone; there was no message from Niti. The same thoughts hovered in my head, when my phone rang. It was Aarian.

"So my girl is ready?" he asked cheekily.

"Mehra, I am going to hit you in the balls, I swear, if you called me 'my girl' one more time," I said, irritably.

"Oh my baby is angry with me," he said, even cheesier this time.

"Screw you Mehra!"

"Anytime baby! Your place or mine?"

"Are you coming to the point?"

"I am standing downstairs, Naina. Get your stuff and let's go for lunch. We will pick up Kritti after that and I will drop you both at the station."

I ran towards the balcony and there he was. I waved at him and continued on the call.

"You did not go to your college today?" I asked, happily, surprised though.

"I didn't want my girl to travel all the way to the railway station carrying the heavy luggage," he said. This was sweet now.

"Aww! You are such a jerk. Come over now, how will your girl carry the luggage all alone downstairs," I said mocking him.

"Yeah right! This is a mean world. Coming!" he said and we moved my stuff into his car together.

✦

We were on our way to Connaught Place when suddenly a traffic constable stopped us.

He was walking towards us and I asked Aarian, "Are you carrying all the papers?" I was sure he carried his licence.

"Naina, I am not carrying the licence," he said with a frown.

"What?!!! Why, how, F**k! Mehra!" I reacted.

Quickly I moved him from the driver's seat and sat myself there asking him to stay quiet.

The traffic constable approached me in the driver's seat. "Get out Madam and show me the licence and the RC," he said.

"Sir, actually I was rushing for somewhere urgently and I almost forgot to carry my purse with my licence in it. Please forgive me this time sir, please," I requested.

"Please madam, you will have to pay the challan. You better come out please," he said adamant.

I knew what the call of the situation was and started crying.

"Sir, my best friend is counting her last breath in Gangaram Hospital, I am heading there. Please sir, please let me go," I said faking a tear.

"OK OK, please go and don't worry and please take care," he said and left us.

I drove ahead for a certain distance and then stopped the car.

"So, you think I have a chance in the movies?" I asked Aarian who was still amazed at my feat of fast, false tears. It was as if I had some inner reserve of tears waiting to be drawn from, quick to caress my dry cheeks when needed.

"You are so shrewd! I am not going to buy your tears ever, you over dramatic woman," he exclaimed.

"This shrewd woman saved your ass today. Be thankful at least!"

"Ya, whatever, there wasn't any need to be that dramatic. He would have hardly taken 100 bucks and would have left us!" he reasoned and shrugged.

"Gosh! You are cheap! I saved your 100 bucks, you better sponsor the lunch today now!" I reacted.

We reached CP and stopped at Subway. I wanted to eat something light before the train journey. I loved Subway anyway. We ate, after which I called Kritti.

"Madam, Mehra and I are coming to pick you up. He has taken an off today to drop us there. Be ready. We will be there in thirty," I said.

"Naina, he is so awesome! Why don't you date him?" she interjected with giggles.

"Shut up and bye," I said, hanging up.

We picked up Kritti and Aarian dropped us at the station. He bought the platform ticket only to help us carry the luggage.

The railway station had always been how it was. It never changed. At many places, it stank like a public toilet. A national urination ground. Red stains of spit from the people who chew tobacco and just spit on the walls and even on the ground without realizing their own kid might just be standing against it. Some huge and scary species of rats and rodents were playing over the track. It was disgusting. The government had all the money to spend and show off during events like the Commonwealth games but I don't know if it takes a genius brain to realise what our already rotten public spaces needed. It isn't rocket science, after all.

The train was supposed to come in some half an hour. I was sitting and reading an article in *The Times of India* about the new demarcation of the poverty line, which announced that any person spending above Rs. 32 in a single day stands above the poverty line! I was about to turn to Aarian and Kritti to discuss this when something else caught my attention.

Two very cute little girls in almost torn dirty clothes walked with a shine in their eyes, discussing what they could buy with the ten rupee note they had in their hand. They finally settled on a Frooti. I was smiling at their innocence. They headed for a vendor at the platform. One of them asked him for the Frooti but he almost shooed them away as if they were some sort of stray animals. Who does that to animals too, anyway? I thought and sank within.

"*Bhaiya*, we have ten rupees with us, please let us have the Frooti," one of them requested, thirstily.

"Get lost from here and don't come back. It is for eleven rupees you godforsaken creep," yelled the inhuman vendor.

Both of them went away with their heads low and I wondered what we meant by calling our country a developing nation? Was emotional, human development out of the purview of development? Could economics alone judge the status of a country? I pondered over and over again. I was numb and helpless. Before I was ready to face this reality again, they were gone. Perhaps, to try their hard luck somewhere else.

✦

The train approached. Aarian helped us settle down and left.

"I will miss you, Mehra-aaaa," I shouted as he alighted the train.

"I will miss you too, baby," he said and left with a smile.

I was lost in thoughts for a while.

"Lost in his thoughts, *haan*?" asked Kritti.

"Oh shut up Kritti, did you carry food along?" I asked.

"When will you ever think apart from food, Naina? Yes, I am carrying food," she said and I gave her a wide smile.

Kritti was so much like an elder sister, an over protective elder sister.

I was so bored. But soon, I found something to pass my time with.

"Kritti, look there. That's a newly married couple," I said pointing her to the seat where two love birds were seizing every moment to get cosy. I was so against the public display of affection and also, I was so bored.

"Naina, please don't start anything. Don't you dare tease them!"

I gave her wicked looks and she knew exactly what awaited the poor couple.

He was about to kiss her on the cheek when I shouted "No" as loudly as I could, and then, a few delayed seconds later, "No Kritti don't do that." The husband looked around to see who it was.

He then held her hand and I shouted, "Leave the hand," following it up with "I need to comb my hair, Kritti."

And for some time I kept doing that until he in resignation, picked up a newspaper to read. I felt sorry for them. But I was helpless. I could have died of boredom. Okay, I am mean.

✦

Kritti finally slept. We had reached Phagwara station. Jalandhar was just an hour or some 30 kilometers away. The train stopped and I had all the avenues now. My bum was paining, all thanks to Kritti for having kept me glued to my seat, throughout the journey. I decided I would just go out to grab some water and chips while she snored. I went down and breathed some fresh air. It was Punjab. The fragrance of parathas, aunties yelling at their kids in Punjabi, lassi stalls, and what not.

I started going to the washroom but it stank so miserably that I returned.

I approached a vendor to buy some water and chips, following which my troubles began. He gave me a bottle with a broken seal.

"*Bhaiya,* please change this, the seal is not in place," I requested politely.

"Madam, you must have opened it, none of my bottles are like that," he said stubbornly.

Now he provoked me. How could he get away with cheating me of pure water? A few people quickly gathered as I yelled and argued and forced him to change my bottle. I went back to the platform and realised to my horror that my train was not there anymore. NO! This could not have happened. I did not even have my phone on me. I burst into tears and slapped my head. Suddenly, I realised that our movies do impart moral values.

I felt the effect of *Jab we met* and was miserable. I was glad there was still daylight. I had no money on me, thanks to the chips and the hard earned water. The next train was in the night. I hit the road. I did not know what to do. I just knew I had to catch up on Kritti at Jalandhar city station. Anyhow.

✦ ✦ ✦

15

Realisation #2

I had nothing in my hand except a packet of chips and a water bottle. And no, there was no Shahid Kapoor of *Jab we met* to help me out. Phagwara was a small town. I couldn't have taken a bus or booked a cab as I did not have any money on me. I had no phone and no money to make a call. Awesome. I was blank for a moment and suddenly something happened. As if it was destined to. I was wandering a bit outside the station, nearer to the main road, when a couple, in their sixties maybe, pulled over in an ambassador, asking me what route to take for Jalandhar! After giving them directions, I instantly asked them if I could make a call from their mobile phone. They very kindly let me do so. I called up Kritti.

"Hello, Kritti, this is me. Look please don't panic, I am in Phagwara still but I will do something and reach the Jalandhar city railway station somehow. You just don't leave before I come. I will see you at the exit gate towards the Ghanta Ghar," I said.

"Naina, you just come here, I will deal with you then," she said, fuming with anger!

I talked to her longer, explained everything and discussed that the best solution was to request the couple who had pulled over for directions, to give me a lift to Jalandhar. Hanging up, I returned the phone to the patient couple and thanked them for it. And they, like good elders, did what they could.

"*Puttar ji* (my dear child), should we drop you at the Jalandhar city station? We are any way going there and you can tell Uncle the way if we get lost," Aunty offered.

My luck wasn't all that bad. I thought, I could do without Shahid. I quickly sat myself in their car, thanked God and then thanked them.

Aunty was talkative, and discussed everything with me, from my studies to my family. She was very sweet.

"Thank you Aunty! In times like these, you gave a lift to a complete stranger. Thanks a lot. I don't know what I would have done had it not been for you," I said.

"*Beta*, you are just like a granddaughter to us, please feel comfortable. And as for the faith, your eyes reflect our child's innocence," she said smiling.

Uncle drove really slow. Like tooooooo slow, faster than perhaps cycles and bullock carts. But what could I have said? I had no option but to ride on a snail-wheeler.

After about twenty minutes, we stopped at a traffic signal crossing. Jalandhar was an hour's drive from Phagwara. It was like the distance between Delhi and Gurgaon. I remember many of my school friends hailed from Phagwara. As I refreshed those memories, a bike stopped beside our ambassador. He looked at my window and said something. I couldn't get it. I rolled down the window and he removed his helmet. He looked familiar.

"Naina Shergil?" he asked.

"Umm, yes!" I said.

"I am Vipul. Vipul Khanna," he said.

And I remembered Vipul Khanna was my crush from school when I was in grade six. I was shocked to see him like that waiting at a red light beside a car I was sitting in, which wasn't even mine. The world was indeed a very small place, I thought.

"Oh my God! Hi Vipul, how have you been? Long time," I gushed, and then blushed. I don't know why. There is this thing about crushes. Even if they turn out to be so ugly and disgusting, years down the line, they bring back memories of when you felt on top of the world. *With fifty students in class, he asked YOU for a pencil.* Crushes, especially the first crush, are always cute.

The red light was quite a long one. Five minutes. I told him what had happened.

"Can I help you? I am going to Jalandhar only for a school reunion today," he said.

I thought if I had to make it to Jalandhar on time, I would have to grab a seat on his bike, no matter how much I hated bikes. Uncle and Aunty were sweet but Uncle was driving really slow and I did not want to be excessively late. But Aunty was already fond of me, and she kept forcing that they drop me but how could I tell them, they were so slow! Plus, she looked genuinely worried. However, I very sincerely explained that Vipul was my old classmate and friend and that I would call her as soon as I reached Jalandhar. I noted her number and hugged her. She was so gentle and beautiful. She agreed and said bye. Humanity wasn't dead as yet, I thought. When you start losing all hope and are about to give up, destiny shows you better signs.

I thanked them for the last time and grabbed a seat on Vipul's bike. The red light turned green and after waving Uncle and Aunty goodbye, I left.

"You have become even prettier Naina," he said. "It is so nice to see you after so long."

"Thanks Vipul and mutual feelings," I managed to say somehow. Yes, this was a task for me. I hated bikes. I was always afraid of them.

"So how is college going? How do you find Delhi?" He asked.

"Delhi is the *awesome-est* place ever. If you drop in sometime soon, let me know. I will show you around," I said and someone crossed the road then, causing Vipul to apply the brakes so hard that I shrieked loudly.

"This was so scary. I could have died of a heart attack," I uttered.

"Don't worry Naina," he said and calmed me down. I felt embarrassed. I hate these bikes, I said to myself for the n-th time in life.

We stopped at another traffic signal before the Jalandhar highway and I saw someone very familiar in a car's rear-view mirror in front of us. Holy shit, to my horror it was Rishab Reddy. No, I wasn't numb this time, nor did I have a sinking feeling, which was good, but I felt nasty, very nasty. I tried to move my hands in a certain way and talk loudly with Vipul and what I said was, "Vipul, don't you think this red light is unusually big," making weird hand movements.

"Ehh, yes Naina I guess you are right," he said, confusedly.

Rishab did not notice.

"Vipul, you know my name Naina-aaaaa (stressing as long as possible and as loudly) is a very nice name," I said.

Vipul must have thought I was just being weird. I could make out from his face. But, Rishab, still did not notice me. The countdown for the green light had begun, I knew, now was time for the final move. I bent forward, tightened my grip on Vipul and accelerated Vipul's automatic transmission bike, taking us straight into Rishab's car from behind, creating a small dent.

"What's wrong with you Naina," Vipul shouted above the noise. I smiled. Yes, I smiled.

Rishab who had angrily now jumped out of his car, was walking towards us, and then, he recognized me.

"Naina Shergil?" he said surprised.

"I am sorry? Do I know you? I said with a confused expression."

"I am Rishab, Rishab Reddy," he said embarrassedly.

I made another choice. Life had brought me before him once again. There must have been a reason. And I could think of just one.

With fresh rage pulsing through my veins, I accelerated harder than ever on Vipul's bike which sped and struck right into the BMW car's bumper with crushing force from behind three times with the anger and ferocity of a young Anger Goddess. Leaving Rishab in drop-dead shock and disbelief.

As the bike, almost recoiled from sudden exertion, before steering out of control, I yelled for help, "Vipul, drrr-aaaa-iiii-vvv-e," and poor shocked Vipul rose to the rescue and rode us back to safety. As I, flew away with my childhood crush on a bike, dropping a middle finger salute to the man who thought he could play with my life and leave without a finger being raised, without an iota of stress. And now that I had damaged his car and shown him his place, a feeling called AWESOMENESS was building up within me. Maybe it was childish, but I needed this one. Even the bike did not scare me anymore and Vipul drove us quietly for the rest of the journey, in silence. I did not speak of the overwhelming feeling of hitting a creep's car and watching his face go white and change colours as I tipped my middle finger salute having freshly damaged his newly imported BMW.

✦

We reached the Jalandhar city railway station soon. I saw Kritti waiting for me exactly where I had asked her to. She was boiling with rage, and scary looking.

Before meeting Kritti, I thanked Vipul profusely.

"Naina, can I at least have your number," he shouted from behind.

"I will catch up with you on Faceboooook," I shouted back.

"Naina, you can always count on me as a friend. If not that, a well-wisher," he reminded.

Where did that come from? Why so corny suddenly? I smiled at him thoughtfully.

I reached where Kritti stood. And she shouted, "Naina, you know Mom-Dad have been calling ever since and I have been evasive. I had no idea where you were, you had no money and you managed to travel a two-hour distance with some strangers!"

"Vipul isn't any stranger, he is my childhood crush," I interrupted with a sorry face.

"Why are you always so dramatic and filmy Naina? Couldn't you just obey when I asked you not to get out of the train? Will you ever in your life listen to anybody but yourself?" went on Kritti, blah blah blah….

"Kritti! I love you! And I am sorry *na,*" I said making a puppy pout. This always worked for me and it did then too. But she started crying. I hugged her. She was actually very worried. She is still such a mom to me.

Kritti had given Mom and Dad the train's time of arrival to be an hour later than the actual. My babe was smart, I thought.

I told her everything that had happened and in the midst of all this, I realised, I had moved on in life. And for the better.

✦ ✦ ✦

16

Could Life Be Filmier?

We were sitting in the cafeteria at the station when Dad arrived. We hugged him and headed for home together. I was ready for a big, typical welcome, back into my Punjabi household. They would treat us like we had come from across the border after many years. And this was when I went home at least thrice every year. Mom was a typical mother, filmy and melodramatic. She would cry and pamper me a lot. I was always a pampered child anyway.

"How come the train was an hour late, *beta*? Till Phagwara, I believe it was running on time. I had a word with you while you were about to reach there. Isn't it?" Dad asked me.

"Yes Dad, actually I almost pulled off a *Jab we met* scene at Phagwara. I got down and missed my train. I asked Kritti to wait for me at the Jalandhar station while I covered the transit on my own. I was lucky to have met all the right people who helped me reach here safely," I said with a straight face.

He laughed but Kritti gave me another stern look. Dad obviously thought I was joking.

Jalandhar was on its way to becoming a city. There was hardly anything in Delhi that wasn't here. Only that there was less traffic, less pollution and better safety. How I wished Delhi was safer for women.

Finally we reached home. The thought of all the cousins together, the Punjabi music, the dhol, the fun had already pepped me up. It was incomparable to any hep party elsewhere.

Mom and others in the house were there at the door. Mom actually had the puja plate in her hand. She poured some oil at the corners of the door and then led us in. Both of us then went to see *Beeji* (grandma) first. She hugged us. Said a few blessings in Punjabi, kissed our foreheads and asked Mom to take some salt and remove the evil eye that must have fallen upon us. How much we loved her. She was the most beautiful woman I have ever seen. Also, everyone said, I resembled her. Compliments!

As we entered my room, *Bhaiya* and Mishti opened the door and screamed loudly to scare me. They had decorated my room. I hugged them both. Mishti was more excited to see Kritti than me. She loved her. Kritti had always been the one who would cater to the most unreasonable demands when it came to Mishti. She was her pampered child.

We slept for a while and got up for dinner. There was a huge dining table where everybody would sit together and eat. Food, drinks and dance, were intrinsic tenets of life for Punjabis. My family was no different. Mom had made eight different vegetables, two varieties of breads, two varieties of rice, sweets and lassi for everybody.

I looked at Kritti's face and both of us could have run back, given the instance.

Mom as usual expressed concern over my losing weight and the long array of dishes spread on the dinning table indicated her resolve to help me gain weight.

✦

Me, *Bhaiya,* Kritti and Mishti were sitting in my room after dinner.

"So *Bhaiya,* you will be a married man now?! How is Priya? Did you go on a date with her after the marriage was confirmed? I was so excited when Mom told me it's Priya, she had always been a great friend, hasn't she?" I asked and *Bhaiya* cut me short: "I don't want to marry her, Naina, I am being forced to do so," and then there was silence.

But here comes the shocker. Mom and Dad were never like this, I thought. I always heard these things happening with other people but now it was my own brother, I was in a state of despair.

"But why *Bhaiya*? Tell me everything," I said and he held his head with both hands.

"Didi, *Bhaiya* loves Manali," Mishti said.

"Manali loves him too. But her family is against this alliance. Her dad is a CBI officer and he doesn't want to get her daughter married to the son of a businessman, no matter how efficient *Bhaiya* is. If this wasn't enough, they are 'bongs'. Without even meeting *Bhaiya,* he declared that Manali cannot marry him. He has been too adamant about this," Mishti said.

"So did you not tell Mom and Dad about it? They would have gone there to talk, I am sure," I asked.

"They did go, but her father didn't budge and almost got offensive. *Bhaiya* obviously did not say anything after that. He did what Mom and Dad asked him to do," Mishti said.

I felt sorry for *Bhaiya.*

"I want to meet Manali, give me her number," I said.

"No Naina, there isn't any point. Both of us have accepted our fate," *Bhaiya* said.

"*Bhaiya*, please let Manali do that part 'oh I am so meek, I accept the fate and melodrama'. You better do what a man in a relationship must," I said grabbing his phone.

I called Manali and told her I wanted to meet her. She called me the next day at her home while her parents were out for work.

The four of us bailed out from home saying we were going for a movie; actually the three did go to watch one, after dropping me at Manali's place. Seriously? I go and fix up my brother's girl and he stretches his legs at a multiplex! Awesome.

✦

Manali opened the door. She was very pretty. Calling her a typical 'bong' beauty would not be wrong. Dusky skin, long curly hair, and doe eyed. She invited me in. Her grandparents were at her place. She told them I was a friend. I went to her room and talked to her. She told me how her parents had been opposing her and *Bhaiya's* alliance without even knowing anything about *Bhaiya* and that they wouldn't ever agree. They were so stubborn that they never let Manali present her case.

We were in the middle of the conversation and I could already see, nothing was working out. Only when I was about to leave, an old lady entered.

"*Udi baba*! Naina?" she said and came inside.

It was her. The old lady who helped me on my way towards Jalandhar station from Phagwara. She came and hugged me. Manali told me she was her grandmother.

"Hello Aunty! How have you been? I am sorry. I absolutely forgot to call you," I said with a smile.

"Manali, your friend is absolutely adorable," she said and then narrated the whole incident to her.

Something clicked inside my head. After a brief brainstorming session, I decided to make use of the newly formed wonderful rapport I shared with Manali's grandparents. I thought, taking them into confidence might tilt the deal in our favour. I told Aunty everything about my mission.

"Naina, I am afraid, but my son is too adamant. I hardly think he would agree," she said.

I was sure she did not have any problem. She had liked me anyway, right from when we met. This instantly put *Bhaiya* in her good books as well.

I called *Bhaiya* and everybody else to their home with the permission of her grandmother. She met *Bhaiya* and instantly liked him. She told Manali's grandfather about everything and he too was in our team now. I asked Aunty to talk to Manali's father that evening and see if anything worked out.

We hugged and thanked them for all their support and then I left. We were now eagerly awaiting the evening ahead.

After we came back, we were all sitting in my room with our eyes glued to my phone. There was no call or message from Manali. And then, the phone rang. It was an unknown number but from Jalandhar. We wondered if it was her and picked up. A female voice spoke from the other end,"Airtel welcomes you to Punjab," and before she could speak further I banged the phone down. These customer care services. How I wish they cared a little less.

Manali finally called. It was eight in the night. She said that her father did not agree. This wasn't good news. *Bhaiya* had at least accepted it earlier, but now I had lit new hopes for them. I had to make it work!

"*Bhaiya*, we have to talk to her father. You have to talk to her father," I told him.

"Naina, he doesn't want to see my face," he said.

"*Bhaiya*, we are going there tonight and you are coming along with me. Please trust me."

I held his hand and he nodded.

Of all the things I knew I have always maintained that one should never give up trying. If anything belongs to us truly, it has its way of reaching back to us in the end.

We drove to her house that night. Kritti and Mishti managed to handle things at home. I informed Manali's grandparents and they were prepared.

Manali's mom opened the door. She obviously did not know who we were. I told her I was Manali's friend and she led us in. Manali's father was sitting reading a newspaper. I told her he was my brother and that he was Arjun. The Arjun Shergill, their daughter loved. Having said this, I could see realisation seep in on Manali's father's face. He now knew what I was talking about.

"Uncle I know you never wanted to meet him. But, with all due respect, I only want you to listen to what my brother has to say. And then you may take your stance," I said.

Manali's grandparents insisted upon the same. He finally agreed after a lot of persuasion.

"Sir, I know you will always wish for the best for your daughter more than anyone else. I stand at no position to tell you that you are wrong. But sir, more than I am sure of anything else, I can say with all the conviction that I will always keep Manali happy. Two people come together because they want to be happy. Happiness is the soul of everything that has life. I will protect her soul sir and shall maintain it. As far as I, a Punjabi is concerned, I assure you that I respect Manali's individuality and will always do so. I have loved her for what she is and will always do," he said this, and looked down. I could sense he was breaking down.

"*Baba*, I know you think and will always want the best for me. But I assure you, you might just get someone you think is better than Arjun for me, but for me Arjun will always be the one. There can be nobody who can love me more than him," Manali said with tears trickling down her eyes. She was on her knees now.

"*Eta ki korochho tume?*" (What are you doing) said Manali's grandmother. "How can you be so cold hearted? These kids are so much in love and at the end of the day; do we not seek only their happiness?"

Manali's father walked forward and kept his hand on *Bhaiya's* shoulder. *Bhaiya* touched his feet and it was all filmy then.

My parents were angry that we did not tell them and handled everything on our own. They were angry, for now they were answerable to Priya and her family but everything calmed down to normal after sometime. The engagement wasn't called off. *Bhaiya* and Manali got engaged. It was all a happy ending or should I say a beginning. I was happy.

Priya was being forced to marry too. Seriously, what was wrong with these parents? She was happy and thanked us. She wanted to do an MBA.

I thought of calling Niti to tell her everything but I couldn't. She asked me not to do. I called Aarian. I told him everything. I missed him so much. His voice did some magic, it soared my spirits.

Kritti and I left for Delhi. I lost my phone during the engagement celebrations.

Mom, of course, cried when we left. Mishti cried because Kritti was leaving. *Bhaiya* and Manali thanked me for the n-th time and I bid everyone goodbye with a teary eye.

"Kids, do call me when you reach back and keep having food in time. Don't eat outside food. I have kept parathas and pickle in your bag."

"Yes Mom, we said in chorus and hugged her."

While I was in the train and crossed Phagwara, I realised how things change in absolutely no time. I was feeling positive about everything. Although, one can't deny, the whole Jalandhar trip was so filmy.

✦ ✦ ✦

17

As I See It Falling Apart, Bit By Bit

I have always loved train journeys, but hate the toilet facility in trains. Sadly, I had drunk too much water that morning and my bladder was full.

"Kritti, I would just take a leak and come," I said and left for the toilet.

Hell! It was occupied. I stood there for five minutes. Nobody came out. Kritti came to check on me.

"Is someone inside?" she asked me.

"No. This is actually some sort of a game. Until your bladders burst, you have to stand outside and wait," I said irritated.

"Oh, happy playing," she said and went away.

I was freaking out now. I was in no condition to move and walk down till the next coach.

"Is someone in?" I asked.

None replied.

"Excuse me, is somebody inside?" I asked again.

No reply came.

"The door is jammed," said a man who had been standing there for quite a while.

I could have killed him if only I was in a position to do so. That creep could have told me earlier. Was he enjoying my helplessness? Inhuman!

Next what followed was a my long arduous journey to the next coach. I had this in mind, that the devil may care who watched me walk like that, and all that I yearned with all my heart was, a toilet.

"Why is she cat walking in the train," I heard some say.

There were a few giggles too at my weird way of walking but like they say, all is well that ends well. Yes, I finally peed and felt quite relieved. The best feeling I'd say. What a relief, phew!

It was evening and we had reached Delhi. I called Aarian to announce my arrival. I was anxious if Niti would have tried to call me. I had lost my phone. She did not even know my new number.

"Ahem Ahem! Even Mom asked to call. So you can always call her too, if you may," Kritti said sarcastically.

"Yes yes, I am calling her. And you better shut up," I said.

I called Mom. Kritti and I then left for our respective flats. I was hoping Niti would be at home by now. After an argument with the auto wallah and paying him not a penny above the metered value, I climbed upstairs. The door was locked which meant either Niti had not come yet or she was back, but gone out on errand.

I started to arrange my things and noticed something rather odd. There was a letter from Niti's diary dated four days ago, addressed to me. I do not remember seeing it when I had left. Which meant, she must have come back home. I was happy. This must be one of those cute sorry letters for having not told me before going, I thought. And she must have gone out to get something for me. Aarian must have told her. I pondered over all possible ends until I finally opened the letter. It read:

Naina, it has been more than two years that I have known you…

Umm... heavy stuff, right in the start? I started again.

Naina, it's been more than two years that I have known you… And the journey had been a great one. I had never felt any better. I still remember the first day we met in college. You tried to rag me, acting a senior and I almost burst into tears. I hated you then. But the next day when you came and apologised holding your ears with a puppy pout you usually make, it marked the beginning of our friendship. Who knew it will shape up like this. You have been there unfailingly through stick and stones and have seen me smiling from a distance in happy times, feeling happier for me than I could ever feel myself. I still remember you throwing a party when I became the college president while I myself forgot what the party was for. I remember asking you, "Whose birthday is it?" Everyone knew you were the most popular girl in the college and teachers had put your name for the elections themselves. But, you did not even come at the day of elections to contest for the post for you knew you would have won. You told me, Kritti had fever. Yes, I have always known this as Kritti had called that day to congratulate me. You aren't a fool proof liar, Naina. I know the past month had been tough on both of us. While you went through heartbreak, Naina, it wasn't just the internship that kept me busy. I did not even go there after the first week. Naina, I was suffering from brain tumour.

I read it again. No, this isn't happening.

I was suffering from brain tumour. I couldn't tell you. I couldn't bear seeing you in pain. What did I do for you in all these years? Nothing! If not anything I didn't want to bring tears in those eyes of yours. I was trying to act hard to move you away from me, but you silly woman, why do you love me so much? You only loved me more. You remember the day you caught me sobbing in the night, that day my reports were confirmed, I suffered from incurable brain tumour. I didn't let Mom and Dad know until last week. They obviously came to pick me up immediately. Nobody knew about this Naina, except Aarian. I asked him to swear upon me he would not tell you. He has been there for me, during my last days.

I was losing it. 'Last days?' What did she mean by 'Last days?' I was crying so hard. I couldn't breathe. I held on to the letter, tight and read on…

… He was the one who helped me out during my visits to the hospital. Please don't be mad at him. He helped your bitch out. Now as you read this letter, I won't be there in this world.

My world ended, right then. Have you ever heard your heart shatter into pieces? Mine did. Right then. I crashed to the floor in shock, tried to catch a breath and read…

I asked Mom to post it only after I left. Naina, my last words to you remain, I love you and I am glad I spent my last days with you. Please be big in life and don't let the grief of my going away come in between your career. Promise me, Naina, you will work hard and strive for your aims in life. I love you Naina, remember me for the good things and forgive me if you can.

P.S. please maintain your wardrobe from now on. I love you biatch!

The letter dropped from my hand and flew away with the air into our room. Into mine and her room. She had gone. I ran into my room and read the letter again to see if I had read it right. It was right. I read it again. And once again. The words didn't change. She had gone. I felt someone pick me up. It was Aarian. He must have known this was supposed to happen. I jolted him back. He came back and lifted me up. I slapped him as he stood with his head hung low. I kept on slapping him till I broke down again. He stood there still. I broke into his arms and cried. I howled like a child. A child who had just lost a sister, a mother, a lover and a best friend. I clung on to his shirt and questioned the universe. Why her? At such an age, why her? His shirt was all wet and I had torn it in grief. I was in pain. I cried for hours. Aarian remained there, silent, he let me cry.

I lost my consciousness, I faintly remember. I got up and thought it was a dream. I asked Aarian, "Aarian, this was a dream, right? Niti will just come over with chocolate truffle pastries."

He did not answer. I started to slap him again. I shook him. I yelled at him. I beseeched him and tugged at his collar. I kept going down on my knees and begged him to say otherwise. He did not answer, still. This wasn't a dream. Niti was no more.

I picked up her picture and cried. I picked up her mug and cried. I stood before my well-made wardrobe and I cried. She did it one last time before leaving. Tears didn't seem to end that night. They had to flow. I went and sat at the door. Aarian came up to me and said, "Naina, get inside. It is cold."

"Aarian, Niti is about to come from her internship. I will scare her with a boo. You go inside," I said.

"Naina, please get inside," he said again.

"Aarian, you go I will get her along with me. You go and make three coffees for all of us," I said.

He held my arms, made me stand. He shook me and shouted, "She is not coming Naina, she isn't coming. She has gone."

I shouted "NO!" I repeated it. And kept repeating.

"She wasn't deliberately losing her weight. She wasn't eating boiled food out of choice. Her black outs were not because of her crash dieting. She was dying. Every day, every hour, every minute. How couldn't I just see it? How Aarian? How did I go so blind while she was in pain?" I said, shouted and pulled my hair. I was going lunatic.

I picked up my phone and dialled her number. Her mother picked up.

"How could you not tell me any of this, Aunty? Everyone but me knew and she just went away leaving me in smiles. I was enjoying my life while she was struggling to live one more day. Why did you not tell me Aunty?" I kept crying and shouting.

Aarian held me. I pushed him away, shouted back again and threw the phone.

I ran to him, held his collar and shouted "I deserved to know; I deserved to be with her. You people couldn't just let those days be taken away from me like that, those were her last days. I was supposed to be with her," I shouted as my red eyes were full of pain and I passed out.

That night I shouted, I cried, I howled, I remained numb, I laughed remembering our 'Who's your daddy?' wake-up calls and I passed out. Niti had passed away. She was no more there in my life.

She had died.

✦ ✦ ✦

18

She Was My World

That night was the toughest night of my life. I cried and lost my consciousness. The moment I regained senses again, I started crying and howling. I puked. I puked over my clothes. I puked over Aarian's. But he remained there. As patient and as confiding, as nobody could ever have.

The next morning I woke up and saw Aarian sleeping on the sofa. I was numb. The thought of not having Niti around wasn't sinking in. I was quiet. Went inside and sat on the bed, by the window. I looked outside, I would air kiss Niti from there when she would go out. I would throw things on her when she came, to scare her. I would throw her wallet at her from the balcony whenever she forgot. Tears tricked down again, but this time it was different. I wasn't howling, I went numb.

"Naina, what do you want to have for breakfast?" Aarian came inside my room, placed of his hand on mine and asked.

I did not answer. He was looking at me. I could sense it was difficult for him too. He had actually seen Niti going through the pain while I was blind to it. I hugged him.

"Just be here, Aarian. Just be here please," I said and did not leave him as I started crying again. I held him tight so that he doesn't get to see my face. I was in no position to see anyone.

"I am not going anywhere, Naina. I am right here," he said tightening his hold.

"Thanks for being with her in her last days, Aarian. Thank you," I looked at him and said.

He didn't say anything but kissed my forehead and said, "I am making some breakfast for you, Naina. Please, get up and freshen up."

There was a cold numbness crawling up within me. I couldn't move my muscles. Everything seemed oblique. The moment he left I turned to my right and there was this huge photo frame on the wall of one of our air-kiss moments. Mine and Niti's. I curled up in the bed, dug my face into the pillow and started crying. I did not want to make noise and bother Aarian. He must have been so emotionally exhausted seeing me like that since last night. I got up in a few minutes and asked Aarian to leave, for I wanted to be alone.

"Naina, I am not going anywhere, I am staying," he said firmly.

"Aarian, I will be good. I need some time on my own so as to restore myself, please," I said with all politeness struggling hard to withhold tears.

He did not argue.

"But I am going to come back in the evening," he said, hugged me and left.

✦

I went to our room and sat below that picture of ours. I kept looking at her, my head and heart were shouting questions in chorus for the first time but I couldn't voice them. With my mind full of memories of instances shared with Niti, I sat there the whole day unable to move. But she didn't come. She remained in the frame.

It was evening. I was still there. Aarian came in and saw me sitting.

"Naina, you did not lock the door from inside. It was open."

I wiped my tears before turning towards him and said, "I must have forgotten, how was your day?"

"Naina, come here and sit please, I need to speak to you," he said.

I went to the couch and we sat there. He held my hand as he spoke.

"Niti always said, 'Naina will break from within after she gets to know about me.' She told me, that you would get into a self-destruction mode and that I should tell you, it was her last wish that you smile and move-on in life with the good memories that you guys together created. I know, it is not easy but you have to do it Naina. For her. We all know death is inevitable, it is sad Niti had to face it this early but for the peace of her soul, we have to do what she wanted of us. Will you not want to do this last bit for her after she is gone?"

I cried and broke into his arms again.

"You are a strong girl Naina. Please don't be so hard on yourself," Aarian said.

"I will try Aarian. I will do all I can to make up to her wish," I replied, leaving for the washroom.

I closed the door behind me and looked into the mirror. My eyes were red and swollen. My face had traces of tears, my hair was a mess. I realised this isn't what Niti sought of me. After washing my face, I went outside and stood before our picture. I promised her and myself in that very moment that I would strive with all my heart to do what Niti had asked of me. It was going to be difficult but that was the only way to make things better.

People whom we love don't go away. They walk beside us every day. I knew Niti must be looking at me from the skies. She died in pain; I didn't want to give her more pain now.

"Aarian, I need food. Are you preparing something or should I remain starving?"

He smiled and went into the kitchen. I opened my laptop and wrote something. It was a poem.

I was walking with the belief
that you were walking just beside
But little did I know
Quietly you had abandoned and withdrawn
While I was standing there
Where you said you will be back
Just a moment ago.

Though I gain strength
From the happy times
We together spent
Of the memories we together made
When with no reason

We would tickle each other
Echoes of our laughter
Rest in my ears,
in my heart.
Tweaking your cheeks
While you lay asleep
Teasing you saying
"Yes you snore"
The way you shouted
"You are a bitch"
I would kiss your cheek
And walk forth.

When we would eat from the same dish
And you fed me with your hands
Every bite meant much more
And I would only get through
Till I was stuffed till I was choked
Cause' eating from your hands
I wouldn't want that to end
And you would laugh and tell me
"I haven't seen any girl eating more"

Broken Punjabi from your lips
That only made you sound funny
You would never stop trying though
To see me giggle and laugh
Those names you addressed me with

Special in their own very way
It felt so much at home
When tired in my lap you'd lay.

But little did I know
You would walk away

A silent tear made its way down my cheeks, I licked it off my lips, right there. Took a deep breath and added more lines,

Though I know if not near, you still watch my back
You are yearning to find out whether my wardrobe is in a mess
You still are irritated to see the house in litter
You want me to evade the darkness and return to glitter
I promise you baby, I will not turn you down
I will survive this storm
I will come out stronger and hold
The flag of our love all renewed.

There were no solutions, no easy answers. You just breathe deep and wait for it to subside. Most of the time pain can be managed but sometimes the pain gets you when you least expect it, hits way below the belt and doesn't let up.

✦

Aarian stayed until night and made sure I had dinner. He went home after that. He hardly left me alone those days. The first few weeks were very difficult. I would often cry silently but immediately I would compose myself, reminding myself of the promise I had made. But it wasn't easy. I would sometimes call out her name in the empty house not realizing she wasn't there anymore. And when nobody would come, tears never failed an entry. I would sit in front of our picture holding my thighs together and would cry. All my friends now knew about it. They would come and give condolences.

"May you have the strength to bear your great affliction."

"My/our love and sympathy go out to you in your great sorrow."

"I/ we share your sorrow, for I/ we have lost a dear friend."

All these words would hound me in loneliness. I would cry each time someone came. Aarian witnessed all this. After a few days he didn't let me answer any calls. He was taking care of me by all means. If anybody, he alone was living up to what Niti had asked of him. Kritti would often ask me to let her shift to my flat but I didn't want to cause more trouble to anybody. I was already a pain, I knew.

It had been a month and my life wasn't moving. Neither did I go to the college nor did I meet any friends. Aarian and my flat were my only world. He would come in the morning, would make sure I had breakfast and would leave only when I insisted and asked him to attend the classes and come. While he was gone, I would keep fiddling with the pictures showing Niti and me together. He would come back in the afternoon and would remain till late night. His parents knew about me and they had allowed him to stay late.

"Aarian, I know I am causing a lot of trouble to you. Please stop coming from tomorrow. I will manage things on my own. I am really better now," I told him one afternoon.

"Naina, you trouble me when you fiddle with her pictures and cry while she wants you to smile. You trouble me when you smile at my face and break down the next moment. Is this how you are living up to your words, Naina?" he asked.

I looked down. I had nothing to say. I was only getting terrible with every passing day. Just then another silent tear forced its way out.

✦ ✦ ✦

19

Of Niti And Realisation #3

That evening, Aarian reminded me of my failure in keeping the promise. I felt I had to make a sincere effort. I went for morning jogs and cooked my food when Aarian dropped in. I had even started going to college after a month. I would hardly talk to anybody and the smile had disappeared from my face since. But I had started treading the path towards Niti's wish fulfillment. Though whenever I saw the pictures, I still cried, silently.

One fine morning as I was leaving for college, Aarian dropped in.

"Naina, you are not going to college today," he said.

"Why?" I asked puzzled.

"Because I am taking you somewhere out," he said and before I could say anything, pulled my hand and took me to the car.

"Aarian I don't want to go anywhere," I said with a frown.

"Will you sit in the car or you really think you can win your way out of an argument with me?" he asked and I dragged my feet to the car.

It had been almost two months since I had smiled. I had almost forgotten the art of smiling. I sat inside without speaking another word and he drove to some place quite far. He never told me where we were headed till I finally figured out when we reached there. A big board read: SOS village.

✦

I was puzzled. I didn't know what it was, never had I heard about it. As we entered, a lady came to us. Aarian went ahead and spoke to her.

"Come Naina, let us go inside," he called out.

What I next saw was a vast spread of land that had gardens and play schools. The kids were playing 'Fire in the mountain'. I was already smiling before I could even realise it. Moving forth, I saw small hutments. Aarian took me to one of them.

We knocked at the door and two ladies and a few kids, welcomed us with the warmest of smiles. It appeared to me like they knew we were to come, for she said, "Come Naina, feel at home," and smiled.

We went inside and sat on a sofa. The kids were five in number. Three girls and two boys. They sat on the floor around me. They got us some water and wafers to eat.

"So all of you live here?" I asked the old lady.

"Yes my child, I am the grandmother of these children and she is their mother. But none of us are biologically related," she said.

I was confused. I asked, "As in?"

"My biological children left me here for I was a burden on them. I won't speak ill of them though. I guess I wasn't good enough. She (pointing towards the woman who she said was the mother) is a widow. Her family did not take her back; she had no place to go to. These kids, are all orphans. All of us have come together and found a resort in this SOS village to find in each other our families and strive to live a happy life. All the cottages that you see here comprise such families. The kids go to school and study. We make homemade chocolates and bed sheets and earn a living. That is how the family runs. We strive for happiness. That is what life is all about, isn't it?" she said with a smile that dazzled me.

I remained silent for a while and looked at Aarian.

"Did you know that we were to come?" I asked her.

"Yes child, people like you, who take time out to spend some time with us, are our only visitors. Who else will visit, you see. There is always some visitor for some family here," she said and smiled again. And it wasn't as if she forced herself to smile but that it came naturally to her.

The kids asked me what we did and were very excited to know that I studied in University of Delhi.

"Even I want to study there when I grow up. Didi keeps telling us about it," said the youngest one pointing towards the eldest girl.

I asked her, the eldest one, "So you are all up for DU?"

"Yeah, I will appear for my board exams this year and then I will apply. I want to study in SRCC," she said and smiled.

"You will definitely get through, I am sure. Just go for it," I said and held her hand.

"What's your name?" I asked.

"Niti," she said with an innocent smile. There was a moment of silence.

Next what happened, not only surprised Aarian, but me as well. I caressed her cheek and smiled, saying "It's a beautiful name."

At that very moment I had come to terms with life and its strange ways. It is as though one has to put in a little effort to unveil the beauty and happiness that lie within a protected sheath.

I looked at Aarian, gave him a smile of reassurance and uttered, "Thank you."

"You are my babe, remember?" He said and winked.

And I laughed. I laughed and picked the youngest of them all and tickled her and kissed her. Their strength made me realise I was submissive. I was happy. I so was. I spent that entire day playing with the kids. Aarian made all of us Maggi and coffee. I learnt how to make chocolates and brownies from *dadi ma* (as they called the old lady).

As the day was about to fall, I bid them all goodbye. They seemed a part of my life now. I promised to visit them every month.

✦

Life was now better. There was no parameter to determine the end or beginning of that phase. No calendar announced the date when everything changed once again for me. No birthday, no new year promised me that feeling. It was an event, whether to call it big or small, I don't know. But it gave me new hope, a new paradigm to the world. And that very moment not only did I learn to live but I learnt to live happily. Something else happened too. Something that I have always been aware of. Something that I took for granted. Something that I thought could not be true for he was my best friend. Yes, Aarian.

My perspective had changed. I saw him as someone else. As someone who would stay awake all night just to play scrabble with me. Someone I could snuggle up to when scared or cold. Someone I could shout at and still expect only a smile in return. Someone to hold onto, someone to look back on. I had started loving Aarian. I had always loved him. From the time that he had held my hand in that club to save my ass from that mad fat guy; from the first time he made cold coffee and Maggi for me; from the time he said rather nastily that I was his girl; from the time he kept awake the whole night just to make sure my presentation was in place and from the time he had just been him – Aarian Mehra. I loved him for what he was and even for what he wasn't. I was in love. I was so much in love.

I picked up my laptop and started typing on my blog again. It read:

I am a nobody to many
But why regret
For one thing I know
Someone would never forget
To check upon my deadlines
Of things important and trivial
Would scold me for being careless
But I would be as liberal

For I know as long as you're along
Nothing I would fear
In worries and in pains
Someone who would kiss away my tears
Would hug me, be my bolster
Assuring an "I would be there"
You deliver a kick to my ego
Shooing away all fears

I can stand against all odds
All I need is you by my side
And if doom befalls
Together we will fight
The break of the dawn
The silence of the night
And gaiety will have to knock our door
Or I will make peace with your sight
A blessed face, with even blessed a smile

My silences are words to your ears
And never will you question
With calm you will take the brunt of my temper
How I worship such devotion

You're the quilt to my winters
Bestowing upon me the warmth of your love
The sunlight in my growing
Completing the me with an us

Every time I walk away
You are there waiting
Cause' you know without you I won't walk forth
For you are the one who will always be
Someone with a forever
Someone standing by me

You're my confinement
You brighten life's hues
I would be in a fix
If I were to live without you
For as long as you are along
I don't care of things afar
For you're my own very shadow
You are my north star!

A week passed. The days in college were good. I had given the internals just fine and the university fests began. It was such a great time. The whole university campus would be filled with students from all over. On the streets, in the colleges, in Kamla Nagar. There would be music, fashion shows, drama, street plays, War of DJs, Guest nights and FOOD. And so much FOOD! I was looking forward to it. More than that, I was looking forward to venture out with Aarian to all the on campus fests. It would be so much fun, I had thought. I had moved on. Finally. Not from Niti, but with her, with life, treasuring the love Niti showered upon me and thanking for each day she was with me, holding on to the memories we together made.

✦

My phone rang. It was Aarian. Something weird happened. I blushed seeing his number flash on my screen. The call ended and he called again. That was when I realised I was supposed to pick up the phone.

"Naina, see me outside SRCC (Shri Ram College of Commerce) in two hours," Aarian said as I answered the call.

His voice made jitters go down my body. I felt a cool breeze just blowing against my face, across my hair, caressing them as it went by. The wind chimes sung the most melodious tune ever and the sunset, from the window, appeared to be welcoming the night into its arms. As if the dark tresses of the night and its spell have forced the sun to bow down and submit to its mystic charms. Everything around, seemed so magical, so pure, so divine and so much obsessed with love.

"Naina, are you asleep?" he asked and burst the bubble of my fantasies.

"Umm... Err... No, but why?" I asked (Oh my god, the 'umm... Err' was back).

"Naina, when will you stop being childish? Now, suit up and move your ass," he said.

Even while shouting, he appeared so cute. I got up and sat before the mirror at the dressing table. I untied my hair, removed my specs, looked at myself and smiled.

I took the towel and went to the bathroom. I shed my clothes one by one. I was suddenly in love with the way my body looked. I looked at myself in the mirror again. Checked myself and smiled. As I turned the shower on, the drops of water glided down my skin rather playfully as if teasing me taking his name. The soap slipped over my body the way his hands would someday move. Caressing me all over. The foam covered my body like a protecting sheath from the evil eye and got washed away with waterfall of the love that was blossoming.

Like a princess I wore my bathrobe and came out with water drops leaving a trail behind me as they made their way through my hair. I looked enamoured and exotic. Bathing was such an experience that day.

I wanted to look the best. I changed into my favourite white *kurti* and wore my solitaire studs in my ears. A little and subtle kohl worked just fine to outline my eyes a bit. After I left my hair open and gave a glance at myself in the mirror once again, I blushed, smiled and looked away. How filmy am I? I wondered.

SRCC was a few minutes away so I went there by a rickshaw and waited for Aarian outside. There was a huge crowd. SRCC's guest night was always much sought after. While I was looking for him, he appeared cutting across the crowd walking towards me. And then, everything ceased to happen.

✦ ✦ ✦

20

A Walk To Remember

Everything around me disappeared. The flock of girls in hot pants, the guys who were stashing their sunglasses, even during the evening, the rickshaw wallah who were taking students from the metro station to SRCC and back, the dogs who now moved to the other side of the road, the car in whose windows I was checking my hair in, everything just disappeared in the air, like a bubble! It was just me looking at him and he descending from the heavens only to make all my wishes come true. The smile on his face left Shahrukh's dimpled smile to shame. The way he walked seemed better than Hrithik's walk in *Jodha Akbar* by all means. His eyes that looked at me, held so much love in them, more than what Dev Anand, Shahrukh Khan and Ranbir Kapoor together could contain while confessing love to their beloved heroines. I smiled and lifted the strand of hair that fell on my lips with my fingers and tugged it behind my ears while my eyes were scouting the ground. I was blushing.

"Hey, you already here," Aarian screamed.

"Why don't you just seal your lips with mine and say you love me," was what I wanted to say but... "Yeah, just reached a moment ago," is what I heard myself utter. "So you must have figured out by now why I had called you," he said.

"Your hair looks so soft, can I run my fingers through them?" was what I wanted to say, but sigh!

"Umm... To attend something at SRCC's fest?" I asked blissful.

"Naina, you are standing right beside the banner that reads KAILASH KHER NIGHT at SRCC. What world are you lost in?"

"Oh really, wow... Uhh. Yeah, I didn't notice." I said trying too hard to sound casual.

"My friend is the event manager here, so let me call him and we need no passes," he smiled.

"And all these people who are struggling here to try and get in, how will they be going?"

"Let's take all of them along. I will tell him we were married and these are our kids. How about that?" he announced.

Usually I would have given it back to him on that poor a joke, rather I wouldn't have asked him such a question, but that day I just smiled. I smiled and looked at him. And I kept smiling.

"There is something wrong with you, Naina." He shrugged.

Aarian then called someone who came to receive us at the gate. I hardly remember his name so let me address him as 'someone' here. He was a tall, huge built guy, nothing less than a bouncer. I know the moment he opened his mouth, he would taste the soil.

We managed to make our way, tearing the crowd apart and walking ahead towards the gate. People were going insane to get inside. Aarian held me by the shoulders and covered me from all sides. The moment he touched me, it was the moment I was transported to some other world all again. A series of day dreams resumed and I hardly remember how we managed to reach the gate.

"Hi 'someone', how have you been man?" said Aarian and took him in a sideways boy-hug.

"Hey man! Hello *'Bhabhiji'*(sister-in-law)," he said and looked at both of us.

"No dude, she is just a friend," Aarian said.

"Oh so-ree (sorry), come, let me take you inside," he said.

Believe me I have mentioned his English in a more toned down way and rather subtly. This guy spoke like women who sit in their colonies during winters and unravelled society gossip while they peeled the peas, more often popping in their mouths than on the plate.

I really wanted to shove something up his mouth. Why didn't he shut up?

"So Naina, what college in you?" (What college are you in) he asked.

"Daulat Ram," I replied as disinterestedly as I could.

"Oh neighbours. You are god to us then," he said and laughed like he cracked the funniest joke of his life.

I got it right, he was least getting my hints. I gave Aarian weird looks and he winked at me. He was enjoying as I was getting irritated.

"I never knew you had such hot friends. I never wanted him to stop speaking. He spoke Oh so well. What an orator. Oh boy I am in love," I said, as he left. I was fairly loud and he heard me say that.

Shit! I was petrified seeing him walking towards us. He would punch me or else Aarian and then his bouncers will throw us out. He would drag me in public and humiliate me. I had imagined all possibilities. Like always.

"Aarian, please call me need if anythings brother," (please call me if you need anything brother) he said, smiled and left.

"Phew!" I exclaimed.

"Naina, I really need to go home the way I came here. As a single entity and not in broken pieces. Don't get me beaten up here," Aarian said sarcastically.

"Like he would have and I would have let him," I said and walked ahead.

SRCC's campus looked amazing. Numerous types of food stalls, game pavillions and contests attended to a cheerful crowd. Lights beautified the place altogether. All that was awaited was, Kailash Kher.

We were standing near the stage and suddenly there was a mad surge of people everywhere. We were being crushed from all sides. After a while, I stood in a different place and Aarian was nowhere to be seen. I was scared now. I looked around but couldn't locate him. I called him immediately.

"Aarian, where are you? Are you all right?" I asked.

"Don't worry Naina, I am fine and I am standing right outside the ground near the stalls. Try to come as soon as you can, all right," he said.

I felt better.

"Yeah, I will try and come as soon as I can," I said and hung up as it was really difficult to stand, forget about doing anything else or moving out.

There were people who were standing over the roof of the college and some were even sitting on trees. I was amazed. More than that, there was a monkey who was sitting rather composedly at the parapet of the walls, quite decent (human) in comparison to the crowd that resembled like wild monkeys. I laughed. There was a guy who was observing me for quite some time. He was standing right next to me.

"Hi, you seem to have lost your friends in the crowd," he said.

"Yea," I said to cut it short.

"So you are here just for Kailash Kher or the War of DJs too?" he asked yet again.

I would anyway get bored till I could get out so I thought I would rather talk to him meanwhile. He appeared decent.

"Umm, I don't think so. How about you?" I asked.

"I am one of the DJs," he said.

I was quiet for a while and both of us burst into laughter thereafter.

"That's a very pretty suit," he said and smiled.

"Thank you," I said. "How come you are hovering and stuck here?"

"I was here early due to some miscommunication so I thought why not rather attend the concert. Moreover, I love Kailash Kher's music. Isn't he just awesome?"

"Oh he so is! I am a fan too," I said and smiled.

The crowd burst into loud cheers all of a sudden. Kailash Kher had arrived. I could barely see him; both of us were not very privileged with height, you see.

"I see someone is having difficulty," he said, kind of considerately.

"Yea, courtesy: the 5'4" me," I gushed.

"If you don't mind," he said and I nodded while he moved ahead.

He made me climb over his feet and he himself toed up. Though we were weirdly close but then I could clearly see the ever so cheerful Kailash Kher as he moved over the stage to take the mic from the Emcee of the event. I was a great fan of his, I couldn't have missed seeing him. His songs were to die for. 'Teri deewani' and 'Saiyyan' got tears to my eyes every time I heard them. And this was a once in a lifetime opportunity, I couldn't have missed it. I saw him taking the mic and his first words were,"Shake your booty," and the whole crowd cheered like nobody ever could. The fan in me died. That very moment. Sigh. I wish I had never heard those words. Seriously, *shake your booty?* I got down from his feet.

"Thank you," I said with a smile.

"The fragrance you are wearing is intoxicating and so are your eyes," he said cheekily.

Now I was worrying. What was that?

"Thanks," I said.

"So you don't want to attend the rest of the concert in the same position? You aren't too heavy, I don't mind," he said and smiled.

"That's just too kind of you but I guess the fan in me just died," I said grinning.

"But you have rather great booties, when shaken they will only give a complex to J.Lo (Jennifer Lopez)," he said with a weird, sleep-with-me-baby expression.

I was worried if I had given him wrong hints. The crowd was settling and I was eying every opportunity to run away to Aarian. I was afraid now.

"Anything wrong? You seem worried?" he asked while I was deliberately avoiding looking into his direction.

"Ah no, I was just wondering when will I be able to get out of here. My friend is waiting outside," I said.

"Someone does not like my company too much," he said.

"Does not like? I hate your company! I can vomit in my mouth like, for real," is what I wanted to say.

"Oh no! I just have to leave now," is what I actually said.

I pitied my predicament. What all had I not planned for the day. I had thought we, Aarian and me, would go out and groove to Kailash Kher's romantic numbers. Will go for a drive late in the night and here I was stuck with this absolutely lusty stranger. I was helpless and uttered a sigh.

Kailash Kher had started singing. The song was 'Tauba Tauba re teri soorat'. I don't know what spirit entered this man, he started dancing. I was wondering if he was doped or something. It was getting uglier. In no time he was worse than the people who danced in marriages after getting drunk.

I would have been still okay if he continued his solo dance but as the song progressed I don't know what made him take my hand to do a ball dance on that number. I was startled. What was going on? I somehow looked around and saw the crowd had settled at the ground entry. The moment he turned his back to actualize another cool move of his, I escaped.

I patted myself for the presence of mind and headed towards the exit. I managed to make my way through the crowd and finally succeeded and exited after jostling for space all through.

I called Aarian.

"Hey, I am out. Where are you?" I asked as he answered the call.

"Right behind you, he whispered in my ear," he wasn't Aarian. It was that DJ from inside. Holyshit! What was he doing here?

"Oh, hi," I said reluctantly.

"So you escaped from there," he said.

"Yea, I had a call from my friend and so I left," I said.

"Oh," he said and looked at me from top to bottom.

I turned away and pretended to be on the call.

"So, you want to go for a drive or something," he asked and I looked at him in anger now. Before I could say something, someone came and kept a hand on my shoulder.

"Hi baby! Where have you been? I have been looking all over for you love," he said. Now, he was Aarian. I felt at ease.

That 'cool' DJ saw Aarian hugging me and left. What a pervert, I thought.

"You always come and save me whenever I am in trouble. How do you get to know?" I asked Aarian and smiled.

"By the way, this time, you left the call on," he grinned.

I told Aarian everything and he burst into laughter.

"Hahahahaha! So you did not shake your booties, Naina? Hahahaha!" he said and kept on laughing.

"I am leaving Aarian. I will leave right now," I said. I was angry.

"Awwww, come here you. I am so sorry you had to deal with that all alone," he said and hugged me.

The best feeling in the world. Snuggling into his arms. How I wished time stood still. I never wanted to let go of his touch but then, sigh!

"Come, I will take you to a place where from you would see your favourite Kailash Kher clearly," he said and held my hand.

He took me to a corner that was parallel to the stage and elevated. There were quite a few people there. Among them two couples and a group of three friends. He said hi to everybody before taking me to the most elevated audience viewpoint.

"You know all of them?" I asked.

"No, I was just randomly talking to everybody," he said.

"Get a life ya Aarian," I said.

One of those girls from that group of three friends said, "Naina, he has been really longing for you."

I was baffled. She knew my name? I looked at Aarian and he shrugged cutely. I smiled. He was so cute. Though he hated being called so.

"F**k you, Naina," he said agitatedly as I tweaked his cheeks.

"Be my guest," I winked with a naughty smile.

"You are so much in trouble now," he said trying to sound vulgar, but failing miserably, when pitted against me!

And Kailash Kher broke into the song, 'Saiyyan'.

Open sky, the crescent moon and the stars, small yellow lights that garlanded the campus, the fragrance that floated in from the trees, the leaves that moved with the wind, the cool breeze, chillness of the winter, and the warmth of Aarian's personality. The two couples who were moving slowly to the rhythm of the song and the mad crowd that swayed gently to the tune of Kailash's magic. It was just a perfect moment. Aarian got coffee for the two of us and was soon engrossed in the concert. I looked at him.

His face shone in the dim moonlight and the chilliness of the wind had made his nose go red at the tip. I so wanted to pull his collar down and kiss him. It was such a perfect moment. So candid and magical.

"Aarian, let's go for a drive," I asked him.

"You don't want to attend the concert? He is your favourite?" he asked.

I just want to be with you and no one else was what I wanted to say but "No, I am kind of tired," is what I said. He looked into my eyes and smiled. He probably couldn't judge the emotions they carried.

"Let's go," he said and smiled.

✦

We reached the gate. There was no crowd. We made our way to his car in the parking.

"Holy cow! Flat tyre," he said and looked at me.

"Let's walk," I said and smiled.

"All right, I will take the car in the morning," he said, smiling back.

It was a cold winter night. What could one expect in December? The streets were not too crowded after we crossed the SRCC lane. We were at the road that lines Ramjas, Stephens and Hindu. The yellow street lights lit up the road. The wind rustled through the leaves as if playing with them. There was the pleasant fragrance of trees and the dim campus we left behind. It was the perfect romantic setting.

"Aarian! Thank you. Thank you for everything," I said and looked at him as we walked.

"Naina, you are the cutest woman in my life and my best friend," he reassured me and smiled.

I blushed and smiled. I was feeling cold.

"It's getting colder, isn't it?" I asked.

He came nearer and kept his hand on my shoulder and pulled me close to him.

"Better?" he asked and smiled. We walked like that.

Yes, there was way too much smiling going on.

I was not in my senses anymore. I was lost to our world, draped in its magic. Of mine and his and our love. We had reached the ridge area. We decided not to go there as it is usually not lit and safe during night. We took a left from Stephens and walked on the road parallel to the Chatra Marg. There was no movement or noise except for us breathing and our footsteps. It was dim. The moonlight and a lone streetlight were the only sources of light for the entire stretch of road. There was some construction going on in a huge building in a vast plot. We stood watching and in the backdrop of a dark black sky, there broke yellow lightning along the building. It looked magnificent. The breeze had something else in mind, it blew and a few strands of my hair touched my lips. Aarian looked at me and before I could move them; he came closer and picked them up from my lips and looked deep into my eyes. That look blazed through my soul. I shook right there. He had taken over me and I was his slave.

Our breaths collided, I could feel the warmth of his breath linger on my lips. It was the moment I had waited for. There couldn't have been a more perfect kiss than this. He was about to bend forward when a sudden stream of light from a truck doomed the moment. We moved back and there fell an awkward silence. Nobody spoke anything. We walked and reached my flat. I wanted him to say something but he did not. I could understand, he only realised it now. It must have been too sudden for him.

He dropped me home and made a move to leave.

"Aarian," I shouted.

He looked back.

"Goodnight and thanks for the evening," I said and smiled.

"Goodnight Naina," he said and left.

✦ ✦ ✦

21

Halter Dress, Yet Again

I kept looking at him. He did not turn back even once. Was he regretting something that might just have happened? Or was he just trying to let it sink in? I was confused.

I went inside and changed. My lips appeared even more beautiful, he had touched them while moving the hair away. I touched them and blushed. I was sailing in my world where it was just him and me. I stood by the window, opened it and let the breeze play with my hair. I closed my eyes and felt it against my face. I recalled those moments of bliss again. It had been a walk to remember indeed.

I went in my room and sat in front of a photo of Niti and I. I looked at her and smiled. I wanted to tell her how much in love I was. I wanted to hug her and ask her if she too thought he would return my love.

"Niti, you think he loves me?" I asked her picture.

She did not speak but the wind chimes in my room made a pleasant sound. The breeze was playful that day. But deep within my heart, I knew it was Niti. She thought the same. I kissed her cheek and picked up my phone to call Kritti and Isha. I put them on conference.

"Guys, Aarian and I nearly kissed today," I said.

"AAAAAAAAAAAAAAAAAAAAAAAA," both of them chorused and cheered.

"But the kiss did not happen," I told them and broke their fantasy.

"What? As in?" they asked together.

"Can you two stop speaking in chorus first?" I said.

"Oh shut up and tell us why you didn't kiss him?" demanded Kritti.

"We were about to kiss, he had lifted a few strands of my hair from my lips and was about to get closer when a truck's headlights beamed on us causing us to part quickly. Moreover, I am glad it did not happen. I want Aarian to be sure about it before anything like that happens. Which he did not seem to be," I said.

"What do you mean *Di*?" asked Isha.

I told them everything about his silence and how he walked back not saying anything.

"Hmm… You think I should talk to him about it?" I asked them.

"I guess you should," they said in unison.

"Hmm, OK. I will talk to him tomorrow. I should give him the night to ponder over it," I said.

"Yeah," in chorus.

"What's with the chorus, guys? Like really?" I said irritated.

And they laughed, yes, in chorus.

"Screw you two," I said and kept the phone down.

I felt better. Now I had to wait for the morning. Insomnia happened to bother me. I was irritated. I wanted to sleep, divert my mind, but nothing worked. Thoughts of him just weren't letting me think of anything else. After giving up trying to sleep, I got up to open the refrigerator and look for something to indulge in, like an ice cream. But there was nothing.

It was only twelve by the clock. There were eight odd hours left for Aarian to wake up, if he was asleep now. I wondered if he too was suffering the same pangs of sleeplessness. I stared into the air, lovestruck.

Then I thought of going upstairs to Tanya's. She had slept quite late the other night. It had been very long since I had spoken to her. My life had become so centered on Aarian lately that the rest of the world had ceased to exist for me.

I called her to see if she was home.

"Hey Naina-aaaaaa," she shrieked as she answered my call.

"Tanya, are you at home by any chance? It has been too long so I was thinking of dropping in," I said.

"Naina, come over. I am having a booze party with my boyfriend and his friends," she sounded quite excited.

Though I least wanted to drop in there after having heard her boyfriend was there too, and to add to the spice, his friends as well, but now that I myself had called Tanya to show all the love and how much I missed her, I had to go.

I changed into some presentable clothes. I least felt like getting ready so I quickly slipped into my green skirt pants and a short halter *kurti*.

I climbed upstairs and she opened the door. She was wearing her black halter dress yet again.

"Oh come on Tanya! What's with you and this dress for god's sake?" I asked her finally.

"Naina, this is my lucky dress," she said and giggled.

"Helps you get laid or something like that," I asked with a straight face.

"Shut up, Naina and come in. We guys just returned from SRCC an hour ago. Saw you with Aarian there, things brewing, *haan*? Come here!" she said and hugged me.

She seemed tipsy already. Even if she wasn't, she would act all tipsy after a bottle of beer alone when she had the capacity to down five vodka shots still standing straight with her feet firmly on the ground.

"Harish, she is Naina. My prettiest friend. Don't you hit on her," she said and introduced me to her boyfriend.

"Hi Harish," I said and shook hands with him. He held my hand for rather longer than usual. I ignored it, though.

There were some four boys in the house and no girl except for the two of us. Tanya's roommate had gone to her home. Tanya introduced me to all of them one by one. All of them looked like they have come right out of the shows on B-grade channels which showcase some sad looking wannabe models in sad contests. The super stud types.

"Should I get you a drink?" Harish asked me.

"No thanks. I don't drink that often," I said and smiled.

"I ask Tanya quite often to quit drinking too much but she doesn't listen. I guess you must tell her. She would sure buy your word," he said as his eyes scanned me like I stood there naked.

"Yes I will, excuse me," I said and moved away.

I was cursing the moment I thought of calling Tanya up. Hell, I wanted to pull my hair literally. I looked for Tanya but she didn't seem to be around. Just to escape the eyes of her lecherous boyfriend I thought of going to some room in her house till she came back. I opened the door of a room and what I saw next was Tanya lying on her bed kissing one of her boyfriend's friends.

She looked at me and got up immediately to mend her clothes.

"I am sorry," I said and was about to leave when she called out my name.

"Naina, both of us are in love with each other. You know how Harish is. He will kill both of us if he ever gets to know. Please confine what you just saw to yourself," she pleaded.

This wasn't love, it was beer, I wanted to tell her but before I could say anything, someone banged the door and got in. It was Harish.

"You bitch! I knew of your infidelity all along. How dare you sleep around with my friend, you whore," he said and she kept listening.

The other guy did not speak a word.

"I love him Harish," said Tanya.

Alcohol, it makes you do silly things. I made a mental note.

The moment these words slipped her lips, Harish slapped her right in front of all of us. I was taken aback. I just couldn't comprehend what had just happened. The other guys stood there like they had just realised they were impotent.

"You slut! How dare you say that," he said and was about to slap her again when I held his hand.

I slapped him and pushed him away. I couldn't tolerate the nonsense she was tolerating. Harish was disconcerted after getting slapped by the girl he was planning to take to bed.

"You are only being lesser a man doing all this and don't you dare touch her," I said with all the audacity and heroism.

He was startled. He looked at me and said, "Naina, you will soon know who I am."

"I know who you are. You are a slut. Now take your friends and get the hell out of here, else, I am calling the guards," I yelled at him.

Tanya was crying all this while. I closed the door behind their back and went to Tanya. She was still crying.

"Naina, I thought we loved each other," she said as she sobbed.

"It's ok Tanya. He wasn't worth it. Not even the other one," I said and hugged her.

"I committed a huge mistake. You guys always hinted, but I ignored it all the time," she said.

"Tanya, our imperfections are what make us human. But once we know what we lacked, we must strive to achieve it. That is the way we live and improve our life," I said and smiled.

"Thanks for being there Naina. If you wouldn't have been here, I don't know what would have happened today," she said.

"You shouldn't have taken his nonsense ever, Tanya," I said.

"You don't know him Naina, he is a very dangerous man. I am just scared of him. You please take care. He can do anything," she said very seriously.

Now that was unnerving. What would he do? I thought. I let the thought pass. I smiled and hugged her. She was sweet but a little dumb. You could compare her with a 'dumb blonde'.

There was still time. It was only two by the watch. I came down to my flat and logged on to Facebook. Everybody seemed to be on vacation, their pictures spoke for themselves. I was so yearning for one. Once things settled between me and Aarian, I would go with him, I told myself.

I really did not realise when I had dozed off, with my laptop on and all over me.

✦ ✦ ✦

22

Of Abductions

It was seven. The night had been fruitfully spent. One more hour and I would call Aarian. I decided to go for a morning walk in the ridge area. A lot of people would be there, besides, lots of monkeys.

I got ready and changed into my track pants and sports shoes and left. I carried my phone, wondering whether Aarian would call.

There were people of all sizes and all ages.

The old ones. There were two categories of old morning walkers; those who took baby steps to make their last days as healthy and fruitful and those, who were seriously jogging at a better pace than all the young lads.

The young ones of my age were categorically divided too. Except for the ones who had come there with clear intentions of fitness and fresh air, there were many who kept other motives.

A few girls appeared like they had come right out of some playboy party's morning walk theme. They were definitely there to impress the guys who strode about in their vests and shorts, weird scorpion neck pieces and a few wrist bands. They appeared to be gym instructors or some special breed of muscular giants.

There were married couples too. Some sexually frustrated husbands, overworked wives, stressed parents with babies, overactive children. The park was the perfect picture of unity in diversity.

I went and sat on a park bench a little away from the streets. Right behind me, an old couple sat on another bench. They were facing the other side so I could not see them. I could still eavesdrop, though.

"You remember the times I would come with Papa here and you would come alone at the same time after tracking my schedule for weeks?" The old woman began.

"Yea, and every time you came across me I would pretend my laces were open, or pretend to trip, so that I could just look at you for more than just a passing glance," the old man spoke.

"And you remember that day when I came alone and you tried to speak to me for the first time," she said.

"Yes, and you snubbed me," he said.

"I wanted you to at least ask again. How could I just talk to any stranger in his first pursuit alone?" she said.

"Like really, after 70 years of my life now, I still cannot figure out what you women really want. You want us to try, you don't want us to try, you want us to be cheesy, you don't want us to be cheesy, you want us to use hair products, you don't want us to use hair products, you want us on top, you don't want us on top, in the name of god, darling, please unravel this sacred secret to me today, this very moment," the old man spoke.

I tried controlling a giggle. Gosh, they were so cute.

"See, I am going to tell you this today, but you promise me you are never going to reveal what I tell you," she said confidentially.

And what she said next was something all of us already know in our minds and hearts.

"Even we don't know what we want," she hushed.

"I so knew!" The old man said and they both burst into giggles.

I pictured me and Aarian growing old. It was so cute. I was ready to wither with him throughout my life. I smiled and started for home.

I was walking lost in my thoughts. Suddenly a car came and stopped by me, the door opened and asked me the way to Mutiny Memorial. I was about to speak, but they pulled me into their car and drove.

✦

I froze. I was trying to figure out what had just happened. Nobody spoke. I was still. They held my arms from both sides. I thought if they were Harish's men. He had threatened me last night. He must have been serious, like Tanya had warned. After an hour, they asked me, "Ae, what's your name?"

"Naii-nn-naa," I uttered as my palms broke into a sweat.

"Ae, she is not the one. We had to get some Divya," one of them said.

"What to do with her now?" another asked.

The one who was constantly checking out my cleavage said, "But she seems too delicious."

Fear crept up my spine. I was praying to god. I didn't know what awaited me.

"Let's just throw her away. We don't have time."

What did they mean by throw her away? Will they kill me, cut me to pieces and throw me in the Yamuna? And what did they mean I wasn't the one they were supposed to kidnap? How does this happen?

"You bastard you think I am some sweatshirt that didn't fit you that you can go and get it changed," I wanted to speak but my vocal chords were jammed with fear.

They threw me in the streets, after a while. My knees didn't move. My body jammed and I passed out.

When I got up, people had circled me.

"What had happened?" one of them asked.

"I was kidnapped. But they threw me off here for they had to kidnap someone else and not me. They got me by mistake," I mustered all my voice and spoke with a lot of effort.

"This generation, I tell you. They will drink profusely and then will forget how and when they passed out. Imagine, a girl lying on the street alone. Anything could have happened to her," one of the men spoke to the other.

He obviously didn't believe what I said.

I was infuriated.

"Look, oldie, just get out of my way and shut the hell up," I said and moved ahead.

It was Noida, I figured out from some billboards. I asked a few people for the nearest police station. I couldn't have let those goons move about freely.

I reached the station and talked to the inspector there.

"Sir, my name is Naina, I am a student of Delhi University. I was coming back home from morning walk when some men in a black Santro kidnapped me and then threw me here, for they realised I wasn't the one they intended to kidnap," I said.

"Madam, thank god that you are safe and go home," he said.

I was looking at his face. He didn't even consider it appropriate to look at me, leave alone lodge an FIR. I was shaken. My lips were sealed and I left the place with my head hung low. I reflected upon how this morning had panned out for me. How from the beautiful ambience of that couple's love I had landed in the world of crime. Today's reality. I wanted to cry. But tears didn't flow. I was numb.

I reached the nearest metro station and crashed on its stairs. My legs gave up. Something vibrated in my pocket. It was my phone. I had almost forgotten I was carrying it. I took it out with trembling hands. It was Aarian. The moment I saw his number flashing on the screen, I burst into tears. People stopped to look at me but I hardly cared.

"Hello," I said, crying fresh tears.

"What's wrong Naina?" He asked, worried.

"Aarian," I bawled. I told him everything.

"Where are you Naina? I am coming. You stay there. I am coming in half an hour," he said hurriedly.

"I am at the Botanical Garden metro station," I said.

"Don't worry Naina, please don't cry baby, I am coming," he said.

I wiped my tears. A woman as old as my mother came to my side.

"*Beta*, I heard what you just said. Don't worry. Take this water. Have it, you will be better. And don't worry I will stay here with you till someone comes to take you,", she offered with all the warmth in the world.

"Thank you Aunty," I said, accepting the bottle from her.

Aarian came down in precisely half an hour. As I saw him approach, I felt an adrenaline rush and charged towards him for a hug. I clung onto him like a child clings to his mother. I cried loudly unmindful of the gazes of passers by or those surrounding us.

"Just take me home, Aarian. Please. Just take me home fast," I said as I cried.

"Naina don't cry. Please don't cry, we are going home," he said caressing my hair.

I thanked Aunty and she asked Aarian to take care of me. When I hugged her, she whispered in my ear, "He looks good," and smiled wiping off my tears.

I smiled and thanked her again and left with Aarian. I kept holding his hand even inside the car, trying to get over the shock of what had just happened.

We went to my flat and he sat with his hands in mine.

"You don't have to worry Naina, never, as long as I am here," he said as he rubbed his hand against mine.

"And you will always be there, right?" I asked with a heavy heart.

"Do I have to even answer that?" he said and I immediately hugged him.

"By the way you look too hot, *haan*. All sweat, a sleeveless fitted tee, tied pony and a red face. Smoking!" he said and winked.

I blushed. "Thank you."

"By the way, since when did you start showing off your cleavage so much. Not that I mind, but just asking," he said nastily.

"Oh shut up!" I said adjusting the top.

"Go freshen up, I will make some breakfast. This reminds me, you should just pay me for all the household chores you get done from me. Definitely, cooking at least. Please start paying me now, in all seriousness," he said.

"So you want to be paid in cash or kind?" I asked acting cheesy.

"Umm, explain kind," he said and I slid my tee from the shoulder while his mouth opened.

"Hahahahahaha! Look at your face! Hahahahahaaha!" I said as he ran towards me.

"I am going to kill you, Naina," he said.

"Try and catch me, you open mouthed dumb ass," I said and ran from one corner of the house to another.

We threw cushions at each other. The slippers were no more on the floor, they flew in the air. I literally grabbed his hair and he mine. We fought like kids.

"Ok ok. I give up. Let me get some toasts for us now," he said as I was about to kick in his balls with a chair.

"Haha! Men, I pity you guys," I said and climbed the sofa to take a bow.

"Shut up and change your clothes. Lest I rape you, for the sweat is making the already tight fitting tee too hot for me to handle," he said.

"Oh shut up, you pervert," I said as I tried to hide a blush.

We did not talk about the last evening. But I was okay, I thought he needed time. And I could have waited all my life for him.

We were having the delicious toasts that he made.

"Aarian, I just feel too stuck up in here. In these four walls. Last night I was Facebooking and I saw someone or the other was on vacations. They were uploading such hot pictures. I want to go out as well," I said making a puppy face.

"So your problem is that you can't upload a hot picture?" he said raising a brow.

"You want me to kick your ass," I said.

"You sound erotic," he said and winked.

"What makes you such a pervert?" I asked.

"If you think I am pervert, you are going to die in Goa," he said and smiled with a shine in his eyes.

"What? What do you mean?" I asked puzzled.

"We are going to Goa babe!" He said.

I was on the top of the world. Goa! I had always dreamt of going there. Vodka, clubs, parties, beaches, sunsets, sand and bikinis, I imagined everything in that one second. Everything flashed before me.

"Who are we going with?" I asked.

"Vinay, his girlfriend, Uttara, you know them right?"

"Yea Yea, Just the two of them?" I asked.

"Yes, two of them and another friend of mine. Divya."

"Who is Divya now?"

"Umm... Divya used to study with Vinay and me in tuition class in twelfth grade; she is a year younger to us. As children, I guess we had a crush on each other, but then we grew up, tuition changed and she shifted to New York, though we often talk on mails," he explained.

Crush? I was curious now. "Oh! So how come she is coming along with us now?" I asked.

"She has come to India for vacations. Her parents are busy these days so she asked them if she could move out with her friends for a few days, they agreed. And then I am the only friend here she is in touch with. She called me and I told her about the trip. She asked if she could come along, I said yes, why not," he said very casually.

"When did you plan the trip?" I asked.

"A week ago. I wanted to surprise you," he said and smiled his cutest.

"Awwww!!! Yaaeeeee!!! So when do we leave?" I asked.

"Tomorrow morning," he said.

"What? Hello? Aarian, I have to ask Mom and Dad for cash and I even have to inform them. I will have to shop for clothes and stuff," I said with an open mouth.

"You have the whole day on you. I will take you wherever you want. The slave is at your service Madame!" he declared, going down on his knees.

He always did something or the other to sway me off my feet until I become his puppet.

"Ok, let me call Mom and inform her and ask for money," I said with a smile.

"By the way, Divya has her beach house in Goa, so we will not have to spend on the accommodation," he said.

The mention of Divya was bothering me now.

"Oh, great! Nice. She sounds quite rich and all that," I said.

"Rich, smart and very sexy," he said as he looked into the air making certain vulgar gestures with his hands.

I was jealous now. This guy was going all gaga over that foreign returned female. What the hell was going on? He could very well see I was going green with envy.

"But not as smart and sexy as someone else in this room," he said and looked at me.

I blushed and looked down when he said, "Me, you know."

"Hah! You wish!" I retorted throwing my slipper at him.

I called Mom and told her about the trip. She was initially apprehensive but when I told her Aarian would be with me, she was all good. She loved him. So now what was left was shopping, and a lot of shopping. I had asked Mom to transfer cash to my account and now was the time to spend the buck. I was pepped up, but the Divya woman thought still nagged me.

From sunscreen to sunglasses, sarongs to bikinis, I had thought of everything that I wanted to buy. New lingerie too, and as Aarian was going along too, who knew if I got lucky. I told myself with a smile.

"Naina, if you stopped looking at yourself in the mirror and smiling like the serial vamps when they talk to themselves, we can probably leave for your shopping. We have an early train to catch tomorrow so we have to sleep early tonight," he said. Back to the mummy avatar.

Shopping was fun. I bought the sexiest lingerie and the hottest two-piece bikinis. I wasn't sure though whether I would wear them, but still bought them. Sarong was what I loved so I could not have let go off that. I bought a bright reddish orange sarong. The one you tie around the neck. I loved those. Like the yellow one Paris Hilton wore in Big Boss, Season 4. How much I loved it, sigh!

The best part of the day was when I had to insist Aarian to come with me while I bought my lingerie. He dug into the floor with embarrassment. He looked so cute when he said, "Mark my words Shergil, this is the last time I am coming out shopping with you," he said officially turning into a tomato out of embarrassment.

"But I thought someone was talking about being a pervert here," I asked naughtily and he grew even red.

"You are going to have it from me Naina Shergil," he said and made an angry face racing his feet out of the store. Of the kinds the kindergarten kids make. How I wanted to pull him near and kiss the hell out of him.

"What can you give me Aarian Mehra?" I asked cheekily.

"You will see," he said.

"I would love to see," I said and laughed.

God I loved teasing him!

✦ ✦ ✦

23

Lizard's Liquid Eyes

After shopping we left for our homes and packed our bags. As I was packing my stuff I was imagining me and Aarian kissing on the sea shore. The sunset, cool breeze, our feet dug into, sand and water. I had goose bumps as I thought about it. I smiled, blushed and kept packing. My phone rang.

'Aarian Mehra calling' flashed. Of course, who else could it be anyway? He was the only one I would talk to, talk about, in those days. My days would start with his phone call and also end with his. When in class, I would keep on texting him and after class we were always together. I would cry with him, laugh with him. I would eat and drink with him. He constituted my world. Whoever saw us took us to be boyfriend-girlfriend. We were that close.

"Naina, I guess I will have to stay at your home tonight as mom and dad are going out and will come late in the afternoon tomorrow and we only have one set of house keys," Aarian said hesitantly, as if he needed my permission.

And now I was even sleeping with him. Literally. No pun intended, please.

"Aarian, do you have to ask me that?" I said.

"Cool then, I am standing at the door," he said.

"You are such an asshole, coming," I said.

The thought that we would be sleeping in the same room gave me goose bumps again. Though I did not have a double bed at my place as Niti and I used to sleep on separate beds, the thought of both of us sleeping in the same room was so sensual.

I opened the door and he stood with a small backpack strapped to him.

"What? You didn't get your stuff," I asked surprised.

"This is all the stuff," he said pointing at the back pack.

"That's it?" I asked surprised as he got in.

When I showed him my luggage, he commented, "Oh! Now I understand why you are so surprised."

I had two huge trolley bags and a small one for the footwear.

"Naina, baby, we are going there for three days. What's wrong with you?" He mused.

"Shut up Aarian," I said and made a face.

"Ok don't get annoyed. You can carry another suitcase if you want. Anyway, look what I have got for you," he said dishing out a large box of ice cream.

I jumped with joy. Another kissable gesture of his. Dark Belgian chocolate ice cream was and will always be my favourite ice cream for life. I could live off it.

"Thank youuuuuuuuuuuuuuuu," I said grabbing it from him. I didn't need a dish, just a spoon, and the box would be over by night.

After leaving his stuff midway, he sat on the sofa, switching the television on.

"Come sit here and eat no," he said flipping through the channels as I soaked in the orgasmic flavour of the ice cream. The sounds I made while devouring it, had always embarrassed anyone who was out with me.

"Only if you put on the channel I like," I said with ice cream in my mouth, trying to sound as clear as possible.

He flipped through the channels and there it was, *Kuch Kuch Hota Hai* playing on Zee Cinemas.

"Stop! We will watch this," I said.

"This comes on television every other day; let's see if something nice is coming on Star Movies or HBO," he said and started flipping through the channels.

"No, we are going to watch that," and I snatched the remote from his hand.

Before Shahrukh or Kajol or anybody for that matter spoke their dialogue, I would iterate the expected lines till my very last breath, a die hard fan.

"Naina, can you please stop doing that. You are irritating me," he said.

I was even better after that. I could not miss the opportunity to irritate him further.

Then appeared a scene in which Shahrukh dances with Kajol after getting drenched in the rain, on the music he plays over the pseudo piano. It is still as intense a scene as when the movie was first released. Kajol draped in that wet maroon sari and Shahrukh carefully lifting those long wet tresses of hers from her neck to kiss it, oh! Jitters run down my spine everytime, no matter what. And with Aarian sitting by my side, the movie was all the more sensuous. I looked at him and caught him looking at me.

"What?" I asked.

"You're beautiful," he said quietly.

I smiled and we saw the movie together. He made coffee and I don't remember when but we slept on the sofa on top of each other. The next morning I remember getting up from his lap when he was still asleep. He looked so cute.

But something had happened when we had looked at each other and he said I was beautiful. His eyes had spoken a different story. Whatever it was, the night was well spent. I slept with him. I told myself and smiled.

✦

"Get up Aarian, its five. We have a seven o'clock train," I said as I shook him.

He grabbed me by neck and got me closer to his face. Butterflies danced in my stomach only till the time he said, "Come smell and tell me, do I need to brush my teeth?"

"You are disgusting Aarian," I said and pushed him away.

"Wear something decent, we are going to the Railway Station. No skin show," he said.

"Yes mommy," I replied and giggled.

We had reached the platform by six. Vinay and Uttara were already there. We greeted them and Aarian and Vinay started reflecting on their gayness.

"Oh guys please not here," I said.

"You guys can take a separate room at Divya's beach house and do whatever you want there," Uttara said.

"That reminds me, where is your Divya?" I asked Aarian.

"There comes my Divya," he said pointing towards a female everyone was staring at.

At a place like railway station she wore sweat shirts, with due consideration to the winters and hot pants. Hot pink hot pants they were. Hardly visible under her sweat shirt, which was open to show off her push up bra and her cleavage peeking out. She wore a red lipstick on her big pouty lips. Ok, but early morning? At a railway station? I looked at Aarian while he was checking her out.

"Hey Aarian," she came and kissed him on his cheek.

Bloody, he blushed like a 16 year old school girl.

"Hey Vinay," she said and shook hands.

"Hi girls," she said and just WAVED at us.

Everything in a very American accent. What the hell?

It was very well reflective of what this female was and how this female was. I looked at Uttara and she shared my feelings while our eyes did the talking.

"I hope I am not late," she said the way Archana Puran Singh would speak in Shriman Shrimati.

"Oh not at all. Why did you come so early rather?" Aarian asked as his mouth watered.

"Oh Aarian, you are unfailingly gentle," she said and made another move to kiss him when I shouted.

"Aahh! I guess my ankle muscle got pulled," faking a shriek.

"Does anyone have water here?" she asked while I was crying in pain, ok faking it was, but that was for me.

"Come I shall get you some water and meanwhile, Vinay, you please look after Naina," Aarian spoke and went away with Divya.

I wondered just to prevent one kiss, how many kisses I bestowed on them with now that they had left together. I was green with envy, red with anger and blue in grief. My face changed its color from one to all as they took longer than necessary to come back.

Why did this female have to return anyway? I thought. I knew how it was going to be for the rest of the trip. I hated her, already. And her American accent too.

"Oh, how does that feel Naina?" Aarian asked me as they came back.

"You don't have to bother. I am good," I said and turned my face.

"Take this crepe bandage, if you might just need it," he said leaving the bandage on my trolley.

Now I just didn't feel but even behaved like a 16-year old. I kicked myself for having annoyed him and felt good about how much he cared. He always did. I don't know what I was thinking. Divya is just another friend, I told myself.

The train arrived and all of us picked up our luggage while Divya's luggage was carried by the two of them. Vinay and Aarian. I looked at Uttara, while she was looking at me. Looks exchanged again and again. I could not help hating her, I realised.

"Ah, Aarian, can you pull me up please," she said as her high heels were making it too difficult for her to climb two small steps to get into a still train. Wasn't just one murder exempt from punishment? I thought as I tightened my fist.

The train moved in twenty minutes. Meanwhile Divya did not stop speaking about her Jimmy Choo heels, her Louis Vuitton bag, her Gucci watch and I don't remember what and what not. Why was this woman so irritating!

"Aarian, you should have booked plane tickets honey! This whole train thing is not exciting," she said as she moved her fingers into her fake curls.

But wait a minute, 'HONEY'? What was that? She was inviting death now.

"I am sorry Divya, but we guys were on limited budget you see," Aarian said.

"Oh come on Aarian, I could have just asked Dad to sponsor the tickets. How couldn't you just tell me that," she said as she flung her hands in to the air and then down.

"We like to spend from our pockets Divya, moreover our parents aren't that rich, you see," I said with a straight face and then faking a smile.

Everybody around smelt the war was on. The cold one for now.

The train journey was nothing special, only that Divya cried of her Louis Vuitton bag being tapered with a cutter, her right foot Jimmy Choo heel going missing and her Gucci watch, well that was still on her wrist. And for the record, I threw her heel at some station while she went at Aarian's berth and sat there. And the bag, I just did that. I hated her, wasn't that a reason enough?

We reached Goa. It was afternoon. We got down and I realised, there was something in the air itself. I was feeling high already. It was a pleasant weather there. Not too cold. So as we got down, Divya removed her sweat shirt and all the coolies came like a swarm of flies to buzz around this semi clothed woman.

"Let's call for a cab Aarian, it is quite humid out here," she said making a constipated face.

"I guess we will get the autos from outside the station, we don't have to wait for the cab unnecessarily," I said and picked up my luggage.

Uttara followed me, Vinay had to follow Uttara for obvious reasons and then remaining two had to follow.

We took two autos and I made sure she wasn't in the one in which Aarian went. Even if it meant that I would have to sit with her in the auto. Yes, that is how things shaped.

"So you don't happen to like me," she said as the auto started. I wasn't too surprised; I had made it quite apparent already.

Yes bitch I hate you from the bottom of my heart, my kidneys, my lungs and every part of my body shouts that I HATE YOU. In your face! was what I wanted to say.

"Umm no, there is nothing like that. What makes you think so?" was what I said.

"It better be likewise, for if it is, Candy, I am really a bitch," she said and the accent was gone.

She stared at me with those liquid eyes. She suddenly looked like a lizard to me. Like she would get her tongue out next and 'lick' me to death. But I was ready for this one. I was a dinosaur if she was a lizard.

"To that, we will see," I said turning my face.

We reached her house. It was a real big one. A mini mansion. The other auto arrived as well as I paid to the first one.

"So, the two of you had a nice time?" Aarian asked as he smiled at us.

"Oh Aarian, I am so much in love with Naina. She is such a darling," she said and winked wickedly. I knew she was up to something.

I faked a smile as Aarian looked at me.

We picked up the luggage and you should consider it obvious by now, by 'everybody' I meant everybody but Divya. Her luggage, as you guessed it right, became boys' luggage too.

As we moved in, Aarian came to me and said, "I am glad you and Divya are friends," he said smiled and walked ahead.

I just didn't want Aarian to feel bad about anything. So I decided to ignore her ways of belittling me.

I was just about to enter the house when Divya came and whispered in my ear, "For Aarian, you will see how I tie my leash around his neck," she said and grinned like a B-grade television soap vamp.

And then I thought, maybe it was okay to let Aarian feel a little bad. If not more.

The house had an artificial beach with a bar at its shore. It also had a gym, a party hall and a swimming pool, if only a beach was any less. It had a servant quarter which was better than my flat and there were some ten house attendants to look after the various chores. In short, it was one amazing house. Like the ones you see in movies. No matter how much I wanted to hate the house as it was Divya's, I was still falling for it.

All of us freshened up and gathered in the dining hall for some food. My stomach was upset and the sight of some ten dishes on the table only made me more nauseated.

"Naina, why aren't you having anything," said the bitch in the sing song tone of hers. "Aarian, I guess Naina did not like the house."

"Oh no Divya, the house is absolutely majestic. I am sure there must be something else that is bothering Naina," he said smiling at me.

"What's wrong Naina?" asked Uttara in concern.

"I believe my stomach is upset," I said.

"Oh my god, candy, you should have told me. I could have got you some medicine," saying so Divya went inside.

"What the hell was going on? Why is she being so unrealistically sweet?" I thought. "And what on earth is this 'CANDY' business? Someone please tell her my name is Naina," I carried on talking to myself.

"Have this medicine Naina, you will feel better," she said as I stared at her.

"Come on, have it Naina, you will be just fine," Aarian urged.

I had the medicine and after a little gossip everyone departed for their rooms. The train journey was too tiring so we all decided to catch up on an hour's nap before going out. That bitch gave Aarian a room that was far away from mine. Uttara and Vinay remained in one room, lucky them, I thought. This was like a mini honeymoon for them. Their room was near mine and her own room was near Aarian's. Did I even have to mention?

I slept reflecting on all that had happened till then. When Aarian went with her at the station, he only wanted to get me the crepe bandage, in the dining hall, he defended me while she was trying to take a gibe at me, so his feelings for me weighed more for me than her. And why there was a need for comparison? While I was with him all along, she was just another friend of his. I ignored the wild thoughts and the tussle in my head and slept, feeling optimistic.

I hardly remember when I dozed off. I looked at the watch; it was eleven o'clock. As in 11 p.m. I was shocked. I tried to recall the time I went to sleep as I felt disoriented. It was still 11 p.m. It was night. I went outside to look for the rest of them and found none there.

"Where did everyone go?" I asked a house maid.

"They went in the evening itself while you were sleeping, madam," she said.

I was taken aback. How could they just leave me sleeping like that and go. How could Aarian have left without me? I was angry; I didn't want to speak to him, to anyone for that matter. I was about to enter my room as I heard some one calling "Naina".

✦ ✦ ✦

24

Not All That Picture Perfect

It was Aarian. He was at home? He did not go? I turned back and looked at him, walking towards me.

"How are you feeling now?" he asked.

"Umm, I am good," I said.

"Where is everyone?" I asked.

"They have gone to a club nearby," he said.

"You did not go?" I asked.

"Umm, while we were moving out, I was coming to get you but Divya told me that you told her you weren't feeling good and didn't want to be disturbed. I just thought I will remain here lest you should need anything. Though Divya said the house attendants will look after you very well, I just didn't feel good going without you and stayed back," he said and smiled like a child.

I was floored. I kept on staring at him with my eyes not blinking. I just wanted to hang on to his neck and kiss him. I so much wanted to tell him that he was only making me love him more with every passing day, hour, minute, second. I looked at him. His flawless face could have put Brad Pitt to shame. In a fraction of a second, I was lost into a world where I pictured me and him dancing in a black and white frame with a moonlit backdrop. And as I processed his words in my head I realised something.

I didn't remember Divya coming to my room. She definitely did not. That bitch thought she would take advantage of my nap and make her advances on Aarian. What a loser, I thought. I decided not to spoil mine and Aarian's moment here with the mention of her so I decided not to tell him about it.

"Aww, thanks! But you really didn't have to stay," I said and smiled.

"Oh shut up Naina! But who sleeps so much man?" he said.

"Yea, I don't know. My head is hurting," I said holding my forehead.

"Come let's go to the beach downstairs for a walk," he said and smiled.

"Ok, let me change and come," I said turning towards my room.

He held my hand and pulled me closer, stroked his fingers in my hair saying, "Naina, you look great. The smudged Kajal is giving your eyes a sexy smoky look and the messed up open hair, fall just perfectly at your shoulders, and this cute little pink spaghetti and your silly pink heart graffiti pjs look adorable. You really don't have to try; you know you are awesome, don't you?"

I smiled and looked down and then I looked at him. He was still looking at me. He wasn't hesitant like the other evening. He seemed to have had conviction in his voice, and I felt it for the first time. And then I realised maybe it wasn't about being beautiful, or not being beautiful, it's about him seeing you as the most gorgeous woman in the world no matter you still were in your pjs, had dark circles and not smoky eyes and your hair looked messy. It was about how awesome he makes you feel about yourself, when he is around.

I smiled at him and closed the door behind my back while we left for the beach downstairs.

We went and sat by the shore. The water surged to touch our feet. That was a moonlit night, an enchanting well lit beach with no people around, little shacks and just me and him. I wasn't in a sarong but pyjamas and we weren't making love but just sitting together and yet it seemed as perfect as it could ever be. Maybe because all that was important was not a picture perfect moment, no rain drops falling on us, nor this beach – none of it was of any consequence – without us.

I looked at him and said, "Aarian, thank you!"

"Is 'thank you' your favourite catch phrase or something? Or you think you look cuter when you say that? Ok tell me, for what?" he asked as he gnawed.

"For having been there for me always."

"Naina, it is my own selfish motive to be with you. It makes me feel good about myself, about life. So here, we balance out. No more thank you," he said and knocked my forehead with his. That was cute.

As he came closer, something happened. His head moved back a little slow than usual. As he drifted away, our eyes were hooked on to each other's, our silences fighting for a place in our vocabulary that didn't help. The breeze above the ocean blew against our faces as if trying to get us closer; my hair came in the way and blocked the view of the angel before me. I looked at him, and a voice broke the blissful moment. The moment when I thought it would finally ensue.

"Hey guys," shouted Divya as she walked towards us.

"How are you feeling now Naina?" she asked as she looked at me faking a smile.

"Thanks Divya, I am good," I said with a straight face.

"How was clubbing Divya?" Aarian asked her.

"Umm, it was awesome! There was booze, there was light and there were boys! But none as sexy as you are. You should have come over Aarian," she said placing her hand on his shoulder and bending indecorously at him true to her uncouth style.

"I am so sorry Divya, I will make it up for this tomorrow," he said and smiled.

"Before I forget, Aarian, Vinay was looking for you. He is in his room," she said and Aarian left.

Now it was just me and that woman alone on the beach. Bitch on the beach. I so will write a book titled this, I thought and giggled within.

"So I guess the sedatives did not work too well to keep you off Aarian," she said as she looked at me with those red eyes. She was furious.

"Excuse me?" I asked perplexed.

"What did you think, I am in love with you or something that I will ever want your upset stomach to get fine so that you could dance your way to Aarian? I had given you a sedative that induced sleep. I thought we would leave while you sleep but Aarian screwed up my plan," she said and still stared at me wickedly.

"You are bitchier than I had thought, and now that you have shown your colours, you will see my hues Divya Kapoor," I said and walked away.

I could have killed her and would have thrown her into the beach of her very own house. But more than angry, I was scared. She looked at me like she would unmistakably kill me. My anger had subsided because intentionally or unintentionally it was Aarian who had goofed up her wicked schemes. I was ecstatic about that. I smiled and left for my room. But sure I wanted to react in my own way.

✦

The next day all of us, except Miss New York – returned late riser, got up early to catch the sunrise by the beach. It was the most distinguished sight ever. The sun rising from the waters made it appear as if it rested somewhere inside and now the tides had woken him up to start the day by sending his golden rays to the earth. The water looked all golden for a while, as if cased in a golden sheath. It was beautiful. God is indeed the most talented and vivacious creator. Such beauty was unparalleled and surreal indeed.

"Isn't this beautiful?" I asked as Aarian stood by my side.

"Yes, very beautiful. I will someday make my house in Goa, a small cottage maybe," he said and smiled.

"Oh, that's so sweet," I said and smiled. "You definitely will."

We looked at each other and smiled. Too much smiling all over again. Woohoo. Uttara and Vinay were walking by the beach hand in hand. They belonged to each other so much.

"Come guys, let's wake Divya up and have breakfast," Aarian called out to both of them. These love birds were inseparable. Lost in their own sweet world.

As we climbed the stairs and proceeded towards the dining hall, that woman came out in an absolutely transparent nighty and sat for breakfast.

"Why don't you change and come Divya," said Uttara, "We will wait here for you."

"Oh that's so sweet of you darling, but I am a lazy girl you see. I will go after food," she said with all airs, quite typical of herself. Bitch.

We had breakfast. Got dressed and left for a day out. Though they say there isn't much to do in Goa during the day, I felt otherwise. It looks absolutely amazing during the monsoons. Cloudy at all times and the pitter patter of rain drops making little water pools all around and the fragrance of the wet mud overpowering the senses with lush green trees was a breathtaking sight.

Throughout the day we went to different places. Fort Aguada, from the movie *Dil Chahta Hai*. Dona Paula, there was something about the place. The wind blew as though it would block your steps. Water lashed the shores. The rocks beneath splashed it upwards. It was lively, enigmatic. Serene and peaceful.

By evening we decided to route for Calangute beach. It was absolutely vibrant. Water sports, tattoos, the hot white skin, the hotter bums and for your information, I am talking about the guys.

"Oh my god, look at that guy! Such a pinchable butt that is," I said as I slurped, while all of us stood inside the beach splashing water over each other.

"You are such a guy sometimes, Naina," Uttara said and everybody laughed.

"And that is why you are still single perhaps," Divya poked her nose in as always.

"Oh really! I was thinking that's because I am waiting for the right one and not sucking every cock that comes my way," I said reflexively, in anger. I was definitely offended by what she had said.

"Relax girls, you two don't have to start all again now," Aarian said, getting a bit miffed. He left. I wasn't ready to go and appease him. I was too angry.

"Let him be by himself, he will be good," said Vinay spotting the frown on my face.

"But really Naina, in all good humour, you are such a dude," Vinay said.

"I saw a movie and got it right, that for centuries men have looked at the breasts of a woman before they have looked at her eyes and have found it convenient to pinch her bum than shake hands with her, it is now the divine right of all women folk to make cheap appropriations about a man's backside," I said with a straight face and everybody laughed. Everybody except Divya, who only made faces in the air.

I looked for Aarian around; he wasn't there. I had started to feel ashamed for having let him down.

I went and sat by the shores. I was about to write 'Naina loves Aarian' on the sand and yes, with a heart around it, but I didn't. I realised, I didn't want it to be washed away by the tides. I wanted it to remain, forever.

I called Aarian, but his phone was switched off. I was worried.

"Vinay, did he tell you where he was going? His phone is off?" I asked as I saw all of them coming towards me.

"He called a minute before. He said he will catch all of us in Mambos Club by the night," Vinay said with a shrug.

I was taken aback. Couldn't he just talk to me once before leaving like that? I was upset. I just did not want to go anywhere. I left for the beach house and all of them went to the market.

After some hours, they all came back to get dressed for the club.

"Naina, we have to leave for Mambos, come," called out Vinay.

"I am not feeling too well Vinay, why don't you just carry on. I will come in a while," I said.

"Naina, we will be waiting and you better come," said Uttara and I nodded.

All of them left. I did not see that bitch's face. I tried Aarian's number again, still off.

I finally wore a red dress and left for the club. It wasn't too far away. As I entered I called Uttara and located them. Vinay and Uttara stood by the bar. Divya was not around. I went up to them.

"You look so hot Naina," said Uttara and hugged me.

"Really Naina, if it wasn't for Uttara, I would have asked you out," Vinay said acting all flirtatious.

"And I was thinking after you guys get married, your first extra-marital affair will be with me," I said nastily.

"That's a deal," he said.

"The two of you realise I am standing here right?" Uttara said as we broke into peals of laughter.

"Where are Divya and Aarian – did he not come as yet?" I asked them as I picked a cocktail.

"Naina, where are you lost? Just take a look around the dance floor," said Uttara.

There, they were. Dancing like some glue had made them stick to each other. That bitch wore a little black dress, actually, the little-est black dress and was all over Aarian. He had a drink in his hand and they grooved their asses at the beat. What was he doing with alcohol?

I got through with my glass of drink and poured vodka in it. Neat this time. I was down a cocktail and three goblets of neat vodka.

My eyes saw something when I lost it all. She held Aarian's hand and kept it at her butt. And why won't he? He was a guy. I left the club and I heard Vinay and Uttara call out my name.

There was a beach outside. I went and sat on the shore. Tears rolled down my cheeks. The supposed Goa trip wasn't exactly picture perfect as I had imagined it to be.

✦ ✦ ✦

25

Of The Stolen Moments

The next day I did not talk to Aarian. We all had breakfast and left for a few beaches and the ferry ride in the evening. It was our last day and I very much wanted to go home as soon as possible. I could not be around that bitch anymore. She had created tensions between me and Aarian. I wanted to go home and fix them. The whole day Aarian tried to talk to me but I did not respond. I had reasons to be angry with him.

"I was too drunk to realise what was going on," I heard him say when Uttara and Vinay were teasing him.

He never got drunk before. I hardly got drunk either. May be that's why I wasn't too comfortable with him behaving this way.

We were heading back to the beach house to get dressed up for some beach party that night. As we reached home, Aarian held my hand and took me to the beach downstairs while everyone else want to their rooms.

"I don't want to go anywhere," I said as he was taking me.

"Guys you people carry on, we will just join you," Aarian told the rest. Divya was giving me cold looks.

So I didn't struggle too much. Worth it, I thought.

"And I am not asking you, Naina," he said and looked at me as everyone left.

"See Naina, I know I over reacted yesterday but I had some tension going on in mind. I am sorry," he said as held his ears and sat on his knees.

Now what do you do in such a moment, when someone you love with all your heart apologises so cutely.

"Oh no, it's ok. Maybe I over reacted too," I said and smiled. *What did I say?* I thought in my head and laughed at my lovelorn self.

We hugged each other and sat at the beach for a while.

"Naina, I need to ask you something," he began in all seriousness.

"Yes tell me," I said.

"Naina, there is a friend of mine. We have been together since school days but it's been quite a while that we fought on certain issues and now I met that friend yesterday at the beach. And that is why I was all the more unsettled emotionally. He has been apologizing and rest of the day I was with him but do you think I should go ahead and forgive him?" he asked.

"You want to get back to him?" I asked him.

"Naina, I don't know! Should I?" he questioned looking at me. His eyes carried innumerable questions. For a moment, I felt as if he wanted to say something. To tell me something but he didn't.

"Aarian, relationships are very simple. We make them complex. Keeping them or not keeping them is in our hands.

At the end of the day, what remains important is love and happiness. If being with some gives you happiness, you must be with them. And as for forgiveness is concerned, I am sure that is not the issue. You are mature enough to understand it costs nothing and brings back some lost happy memories," I said and smiled.

He hugged me the moment I said this.

"What would I do without you Naina?" he said and I smiled.

"Now will you make this friend of yours meet us as well?" I asked. "Why don't you get him along?"

"I will, tonight. And that will be a surprise for you," he said and I looked at him with curiosity.

✦

All of us got dressed and left for the beach party at Palolem Beach. I took longer than necessary to get dressed. I had decided to wear the sarong. With hair open and lots of kohl, I got downstairs. Aarian was there waiting for me while the rest had left by one of the cabs.

"You are making me stiff," he said and looked at me open mouth.

"Gosh that is gross, Aarian," I said and nudged him away.

"Naina, you are looking like some Greek goddess who has descended upon the earth to satiate the eyes of all those who never knew what beauty meant in its true senses," he said still gaping.

"What makes you so sweet and all pepped up today?" I asked as I blushed.

"That's a surprise awaiting you baby," he said and we left for the beach.

As we got down what I saw was the whole space illuminated with amazing lights and from discos to lounge bars to restaurants to beach shacks, there was everything to keep the night on fire and of course, there was booze. It flowed like water. It was one of the most outlandish sights abuzz with music and booze.

"Naina, just come here," he called out. He had a big white lily in his hand and he placed it behind my ear.

"Thanks, I look way better with this!" I said as I smiled.

"No, the lily looks better now," he said and smiled back.

A look into each other's eyes and we headed towards the party space and located Vinay and Uttara.

Divya was drunk already and was dancing with one of the foreigners there. Not a hot one, though. Well deserved, I thought and felt great.

Vinay spoke as he saw me and Aarian coming "You guys should just start dating each other," he was a little tipsy.

I smiled and looked at Aarian, he did not seem to have heard it. He was looking somewhere in the crowd.

"Where are you looking at?" I asked.

"Oh nothing, come let's dance," he said and took me by the arm before I could say anything.

He held me by the waist and pulled me towards himself. Our bodies collided and we almost felt each other's breath. A goblet of whiskey down and we were dancing even nastily. I slid over his body like a snake and he played with me like I was a rope. My hair was all around the place and his hands holding me by the waist as we grooved. After a while, all the people there looked at us but we were unaware of what was happening. We were lost, into the music of each other's soul, heart beats and breath.

"You want to go to the beach," he shouted in my ear. The music was too loud to hear anything otherwise.

"Yes," I shouted back.

We managed to walk our way till the beach. A little away from where the party was. The moment we reached there both of us tripped down. We laughed our asses off and then lay on the shore.

"The sky is so clear. Full of stars. Isn't it beautiful?" I said.

"It's amazing," he said.

"I never knew you dance so well," I said and looked at him.

"I was only trying to not lose myself, you burnt the dance floor," he said as he touched my forehead with his hands to wipe away the sweat that covered it.

It was such a sweet moment. We both looked into each other's eyes and remained there. I don't know what was on his mind, but for me, I no longer wanted to go home.

We lay there and it soon started drizzling. I got up and he held my hand, "You really want to leave?" he asked.

He got up and held me by the waist. We danced a salsa, a tango, a ball dance and the ever so boisterous Govinda *chaap* dance as we sang aloud songs. Sometimes, we just don't need anyone else but someone who sculpts perfection into the most imperfect things. Sometimes it is about creating your perfect moment.

We danced our hearts out. It had started to pour heavily now.

"Aarian, you had to give me some surprise this evening," I asked gaping.

"Yea, I had to but that remains postponed for tomorrow. And before you leave you will know," he said.

After the rain stopped Uttara, Vinay and Divya came towards us.

We lighted a bonfire and sat around.

"Naina, you are such a bitch, I hate you. Of all the times I tried to keep you off Aarian...," Divya spoke all of a sudden and passed out. Had it been any other day it would have bothered me but not so that night, I didn't even care a rat's ass.

We laid her at one of the shacks.

We remained up through the night and enjoyed our last few moments in Goa. Vinay and Uttara were inseparable as ever, Divya lay asleep. Aarian was enjoying the night singing some Kishore Kumar numbers. He was his favourite and I looked at him with all the love in my eyes. I looked at all of them and realised, there is nothing bad in the world if we know how to figure out the good out of it.

It was the best night of my life, one of the most beautiful ones. I thought if I will ever get to live this ever again, if I ever will see these people together like this, around a bonfire, with the sea ahead, an open blue star studded sky and him, Aarian.

✦ ✦ ✦

26

Of Heels, Sprains And Kisses Undone

The next day we left for Delhi. The train journey was pleasant and relatively quiet. Divya continued to act all smart, but this time, she did not get her way. Ever since her private confession about trying to keep me and Aarian apart purposely, everyone had kept themselves at bay from her and her schemes.

We were about to reach Delhi early in the morning, when Priyanka from the fashion society of my college called me.

"Hey Naina, how have you been? Good time to talk?" she inquired.

"Hi Priyanka, yes tell me what's it?" I said.

"Naina, actually we have a performance tomorrow at Hindu College and one of our team members cannot make it due to some family issues. I was wondering if you can just make it for tomorrow's show. I will be really thankful!" she asked.

"But how will I pick up the choreography in a day?" I puzzled aloud.

"Naina, there is nobody as polished as you are. And you know that," she said and got a smile on my face.

God, I was such a Leo. You praise them once and the lioness becomes a little kitten purring her way to your word.

Besides, Priyanka was someone I had always loved. She was admirable, adorable and sweet. She was one of those people who wouldn't be all over you all the time but would certainly be by your side when you needed them. I couldn't have said no!

"Ok Priyanka, I am game. But what about the clothes and everything?" I asked.

"You don't have to worry. We have a black backless gown for you with wings to go with it. Also, you will be the show stopper for the day. The theme is 'Insomnia'. Good with you?" she asked.

"Awesome it is," I said.

"Cool then! Can I expect you in the college at two o'clock in the afternoon today?" she said.

"Yes I will be there," I said and hung up.

The feeling of being a show stopper had already set free butterflies in my stomach. I have always wondered about how it felt to hit the ramp. A huge crowd roaring as you arrive and the lights fall on you. I had always taught girls the catwalk during the Miss DRC contest but then being a part of the fashion team was something I had never imagined. Taking part in a single show was good enough for me. It was a wish fulfillment in disguise.

"So now madam is going to do modelling," said everyone in a sing song.

"Shut up guys, it's just about one show. And all of you must come," I said blushing.

I realised Divya had been sitting alone away from us. I did not quite like it. All of us celebrated as a group and she was silent in one corner of the berth. Even if things were ugly, her silence was bothering me. She looked better at her bitchy best, I thought.

As everyone expressed excitement over my fashion show programme, I noticed Divya move towards the compartment's gate. I did not quite like the situation now. I never had foes nor did I want any. Moreover, we had ignored her enough. She was feeling so left out, I could see from her face. I thought I would just try and break the ice and mend things.

I went after. She stood there alone smoking a Marlboro off. She looked melancholic and sunken.

"Naina, you know I always despised you, for you were so pretty and everyone loved you. I wanted to be loved. My insecurities once again have led me to lose the few friends I had. Aarian now thinks I am a bitch," she said and a tear rolled down her cheek.

"Divya, you are very very sexy and please don't feel insecure about anything," I extended my hand forward and she came to hug me.

"Divya, I would really like if you could come to the fashion show," I said as we hugged.

"Umm, ya, I guess I am busy, but I will try," she said and we both laughed.

I realised a little love is what all of us crave for. You give love, you get it back.

We reached the station. It was the best trip of my life. The morning walks, the fights, the laughter, the tears, all the moments when I danced with Aarian, the moment when I lay in the sand under the vast sky with him, the sight of love birds all around, the beauty of the sea, the sunrise at the beach everything now had come to an end.

Everyone hugged each other and Divya came and hugged me again.

"Aarian looks best with you. And happiest too," she whispered in my ear.

Both of us smiled. It was always so cute to hear such things about me and him and from someone who was up against us sometime back. It felt as if he was now a part of me. He certainly was.

"Guys my car is coming, so I will drop all of you," Divya said.

How a little effort from my end had changed everything, I thought. Divya wasn't any less spoilt now but she was not a bitch anymore.

We waited for a while at the station and recalled all the Goan crazy moments. It was such a gratifying experience. Everybody shared the view that the memories of the past few days would always bring smiles to our faces.

Divya's car came and she dropped everybody at their door steps. In the end she dropped me. I hugged her as I left. As I climbed the stairs of my house she came out of her car and called out, "Naina, you are the prettiest girl I have ever come across in my life."

"And you are the hottest baby," I shouted.

I waved her goodbye and she left.

After a good sleep I got up and looked around for my mobile. I called Isha and Kritti to tell them about the fashion parade. I wanted everyone to come as this would be my first and last attempt at something so glamorous. All of them were so excited about it.

I carried my heels for the practice and left for the college wearing my Palazzo pants and tee.

As soon as I reached the centrestage, all the team members shouted at the pitch of their voices. They loved me like anything. Out of the team of ten, six were the ones I had taught the subtle and savvy nuances of catwalking when they had participated in the Miss DRC contest. They were elated to watch me today.

Priyanka and Palak were my best of friends here. Had it not been for them I would not have joined them for the grand day.

"Hey guys," I greeted happily.

"I am so glad you came," said Palak.

"Oh come on! Anything for you guys," I said and smiled.

"Naina, this is your attire for the show tomorrow," Priyanka said as she handed me the bag.

"Can I just see it once?" I asked.

"Of course, Naina," Priyanka said with a smile.

It was a flowy black satin tube gown. It was backless and all corset from behind. There were black wings to be worn with it and a black diadem for a head gear. I already could feel the ramp below my feet. I was swayed seeing the dress.

"This is beautiful guys! You guys have really done a nice job," I said as I looked at both of them and they smiled.

"Today is the dress rehearsal girls. After we brief Naina the choreography and practise with her, we will switch to the 'Insomnia' attire," Priyanka said.

"Everybody on your heels," said Palak and the girls got going.

I saw them sway their asses with such poise, their legs worked in sync as if they were programmed to walk that way: so masterful and yet so lively. The track was an instrumental trance number. The whole mood was so sensual that I got on my toes to join them and walk. In about fifteen minutes, I was perfect in my entry and we practised for about an hour after that.

I went to the washroom and switched to the black enigmatic garment as everyone went to change into theirs. I looked at myself in the mirror. It was phenomenal. My curves, my white skin, everything was so well complimented by this beautiful piece of clothing that embraced my body.

"You look overwhelming Naina," said Priyanka as she looked at me.

"Admirable indeed," said Palak.

"Not better than you guys," I said and smiled.

"Come girls lets practise now. All of you look great," called out Priyanka.

It was amazing to walk in that amazing flowy dress but I knew it would be unmanageable, though I somehow started. I managed the first entry great!

"Great going Naina," shouted Priyanka as I made my solo entry and the moment I kept my next step ahead, I tripped.

"Guys, first aid," shouted Priyanka as she saw me trip.

Everyone came running by as I cried in pain. There was actually something with me and tripping, I thought.

"Come get up Naina, hold my hand," said Palak.

"Ahhh, I cannot," I said trying.

After that they somehow managed to lift me up and took me to the common room.

"Guys don't worry I will manage tomorrow's show. I will see you in the morning but now, I guess, I should leave," I said.

"Oh of course Naina, and by the night if you don't feel good enough, no worries, we will see and do something but don't ignore the pain. Come only if you feel all right, ok," said Priyanka worrying.

"Oh Priyanka you're adorable and I will make it for sure. I want to do this," I said and hugged her.

I called Aarian and asked him to pick me up. I couldn't have moved on a rickshaw.

He turned up in twenty minutes and the girls remained with me till I left.

"God it's hurting too much," I said as Aarian helped me walk to the car.

"I guess we should visit a doctor lest it's something serious," he said.

"Oh for god's sake, it's just a sprain," I said.

"I didn't ask for your pea sized brain's take on it. I am telling you, we have to go," he insisted.

I felt like eating him up.

We went to the doctor's and he said, "I guess a fashion parade and heels should be something you shouldn't even think about. It's a muscle tear."

And there it was, Aarian was going all berserk about it. We came back home and all the way through I was only pleading with him to let me go forth with the show.

"You are not doing the show tomorrow. End of discussion, Naina," he said.

"Aarian please, it's just about ten minutes on the stage and then I will be through," I said.

"Nothing doing," he said with all the firmness in his voice and turned away.

"Aarian, it's my last year in college, I will never see these people ever again, you will leave the country for your film appreciation course, and life is going to change. Before that please just let me make most of the opportunities that fall my way, please," I said making a puppy pout. And yes, it worked once again.

"OK, but we are leaving for your home and you are drinking turmeric milk. And I am coming along to keep a check," he said and I agreed like a good girl.

He gripped me by the shoulder from behind and helped me climb the stairs somehow and when it failed, he carried me on his back. Just for this treatment, how I wished there was a muscle tear at least once every week!

"This is disastrous; I will die Aarian if I had another sip of this milk," I said as I sipped the turmeric milk. It was disgusting.

"Your call Naina, don't participate then," he said.

I drank the glass of turmeric milk and quickly put in some pieces of dark chocolate in my mouth to change the taste. The world should be made of dark chocolates. Aren't they just awesome?

He got Volini and applied it on my ankle. I took out my digicam and we looked at some Goa pictures together and laughed. There were moments when both of us quietly looked at each other at the mention of the night when we were alone at the beach at Divya's house for some time. Those few hours gave us something, some memories and some feelings which I was sure weren't one sided. I saw something in his eyes, something that he couldn't say, something that I wanted him to say.

He made *Rajma Chawal* (kidney beans and rice) for the two of us later.

"Umm, it is delicious," I said as I gorged over it like beggars.

"Thank you sweety," he said as we ate.

It was late night and the weather was getting cold. It had even started pouring outside.

"Aarian, why don't you just stay here tonight? It is pouring heavily outside," I said, though my eyes said something else. I wanted him to be mine that night.

"Umm, No Naina, I guess I should leave," he said. I didn't know if he had read them.

That was weird and indifferent. After the incident at the beach he had started behaving unusually and now he wanted to go. Why? Was I interpreting it all wrong?

"Uhh, I am leaving. You take care okay," he said and made a move to leave.

I got up to ask him to stay and my ankle twisted again, but this time he was just in time to catch me. He held me by the waist and we were as close as we could ever be. I had grabbed his back by both my hands. My hands caressed his back and his mine as we tried to firm our feet on the floor. Our noses brushed against each other's and then we paused. The breaths went heavy. I could feel his breath on my lips. He got closer and before I could part my lips to touch his, he moved back. Why, again this hesitation? Why now? I thought to myself.

There was an awkward silence and he helped me get back to my bed.

"Naina, really, don't keep dancing around and sleep," he said trying to sound normal.

He left and from the door spoke, "By the way, the surprise is due for tomorrow. I don't know if that's a surprise anymore, but that's something you should know," he said and left.

I had been so taken over by the whole Hindu fashion parade that I had completely forgotten about Aarian's surprise. It was definitely something big as Aarian was harping on about it so often.

Why on earth didn't guys understand that a girl cannot handle curiosity. And that too when this comes from someone you love? I texted Priyanka and Palak that I would come to the show and managed to sleep somehow despite all the curiosity creating unrest in my mind and body.

✦ ✦ ✦

27

Was I Dreaming?

The next morning Priyanka picked me up from the flat. She had come in one of the member's cars.

"How are you feeling now?"she asked.

"Better, but I guess I will walk there alone now and not practise. I mustn't stress my ankle too much. And don't worry, I won't let you down," I said and smiled.

"You will only do better Naina, I know. You don't have to mention this and thanks for coming," she said putting one hand on my shoulder with great reassurance.

The team practised for some time and then we left for Hindu. Aarian, Vinay, Divya and Uttara were standing right there. I hugged all of them as they wished me luck.

"Aarian, what's the surprise?" I asked.

"After your show, Naina," he said and went inside the auditorium.

Isha and Kritti were already inside. They knew each other through me and were cherishing each other's company. That is how my friends have to adjust. I have some in all groups always. I called them out, met them and went to the green room. Ours was the last slot for the performance.

We changed with ease and got dressed up. I couldn't believe my eyes but I had never looked better. I missed Niti that moment, a lot. She always asked me to get into the fashion society and satin gowns were the ones she was always crazy about. She would have loved to see me like this. But I knew she still must have been looking at me, from up there. I smiled and made a pout in the mirror with all the airs and felt like a model. And air-kissed the sky. For Niti.

The curtains were raised and the announcements made.

"Please welcome the next team that will sway your hearts, team DEBONAIR, the fashion society of DAULAT RAM COLLEGE," and the crowd cheered fanatically.

The music was turned on and the lights, dimmed. We hit the ramp and we burnt it. The crowd went into a frenzy and went up in raptures, roaring and hooting for us at the top of their lungs. When my solo walk came, I lifted my gown from both sides like a princess and walked. I saw nothing, not the crowd, not anybody else but myself. I was again transported to my fancy. Sitting in the audience I saw myself, feeling happy that I had done what I always wanted to. And next to me sitting was him, Aarian. He held my hand and both of us seemed so much in love. At that very moment, I knew I would just go and tell him that I loved him. I had decided, first thing after the show, would be this. I am going to say it out loud to him. I was driven towards love like never before, I couldn't have waited now. I had to tell him.

The show was great. I was full of zeal and so was the team.

After all the teams had performed, it was time to judge the best female and male models. And the cheer, the whistles and the roar of the crowd when they announced "Naina Shergil" still echoes in my ears today.

The results were announced. Debonair had won second place in the fashion parade and the best female model was awarded to "NAINA SHERGIL!". Yes, I had done it.

Many hands came forward to congratulate me but I wanted to hold only one. His. Aarian's. I changed back into my clothes and rushed to locate him. From a distance I saw him talking to someone. The expression on his face was rather serious. I went ahead to find out who that was.

There stood a plump woman, wheatish complexion and short hair. I paused to recollect if I knew her. No, she was none of my common friends with him. Suddenly they hugged, for longer than usual. I felt uncomfortable about it. It sure was something else. I moved a little towards them to a place from where they couldn't see me and I could eavesdrop on their conversation.

"Trishala, I am glad I finally came across you in Goa and after speaking to Naina, I am even clear about it in my head," spoke Aarian.

Wasn't it a HE and not SHE he talked to me about in Goa?! I pondered.

"I couldn't have been happier, Aarian. I guess this was just meant to be," she said and held his hands. "Ok, now you got to show me what you have been writing down there," she said pointing to a diary in his hand.

And then what happened took me by storm. I stood there with my eyes fixed on them, I felt molten hot iron flowing in my ears. Aarian opened the diary and read out loud:

"The first day that I ever saw you, it took me some seconds to realise I was still on earth. You looked beyond the universe. The first time you ever held my hand, I literally missed a beat. Of every time I felt your breath on my skin it took me hard to have kept away from you. Need I say I have pictured you in my growing? Before I knew you, I never thought someone could ever be this captivatingly beautiful with the most piercingly beautiful eyes. They reflect on the person you are from inside, and I love you for that. I don't want to be left here thinking if you said a no, what would my life be like; I don't want to keep this to myself only because some 'what ifs' and 'buts' bother me. I am sure there are a hundred out there who would love you, but I promise you, none would love like me. I love you. I love you a lot!"

And there was more to it, but the moment I heard him announce his love to her, all I heard was "Blah blah blah blah."

A huge crowd rushed through the auditorium and I didn't realise when I had reached Hindu's gate.

Was it all just only in my head then? Was he just too saintly to keep awake during nights for just another friend? The look that we shared when he told me he had to leave for New York State University, the sentiments that got built up, was it all then just the figment of my imagination that I thought he was reciprocating my love and desire for him? That day after the SRCC concert, during that ever so perfect walk, when he stood half an inch away from my lips, was I bloody harbouring these feelings alone? The way we lay at the beach in Goa, the way he looked at me, the way he held me and danced? Was I dreaming? The worst part, I was the one behind their getting together? It is my advice that worked for the two of them?

"Aarian, forgiving is all a bull shit idea, undo your decision. I am the one," I wanted to say but words stayed anchored in my throat.

Why did they ever meet in Goa? Why did she ever have to get back? Why couldn't she just leave Aarian for me? I was numb.

I just did not want to see anybody. I turned my phone off and ran towards a rickshaw and he dropped me at Bungalow Road. I hardly remember if I even asked him to do so. I was just sitting silently lost in the abyss of dejection. I was numb. Tears knew no end. The last time I cried like this was when Niti passed away. The world ceased to exist for me in those moments. I went and sat at Barista, on one of the tables that lay outside.

With my hands on my head I was looking down crying. Why did God have to choose me for all the depravity? A best friend who was no less than a sister and now another best friend whom I was in love with?! Their faces flashed before my eyes one by one. The moments that I had spent, air kissing Niti, her cleaning my wardrobe, dancing with Aarian, those moments when I thought he would just kiss me, the times when he lifted those strands of hair from my face. At one side stood Niti, waving me goodbye and at the other stood Aarian with Trishala. I looked at them and silent tears surged their way out. Like a little child who lost his favourite toy, I stood there with eyes begging for reasons to smile. I struggled hard to shove these images from my head in vain. I witnessed my plight helplessly with every muscle jammed, every breath borrowed and every sight pricking my soul.

I looked around and there were places that reminded me of him. People appeared to pity my fate. I was lost. I was numb. Again.

"Didi," a voice interrupted my thoughts, tugging at my emptiness.

I looked at my side, clinging to the grill were Salman and Shabana. Yes, those very two kids I had first met when I was with Aarian outside Domino's. Another memory that made me stand before him. Everything around was shouting his name in my ears.

I wiped my tears and asked them to come and sit beside me.

"How are you two?" I asked.

They both put their hands forward; one held a Belgian chocolate ice cream cup and the other a few paper chits in hand.

Shabana held her arm out with a spoon full of ice cream as I wiped my tears and had it. Salman handed over those chits to me. As I went through them, I found bills from CCD, Barista, Costa, Domino's and many other places. One of them fell from my hand and I saw something written behind it.

"October, meeting one, Naina looked beyond words. Is she real?" on a CCD bill.

"She is magical. Everyone just wants to be with her. Me too," read another CCD bill.

There were many like these and then I read a few more, "Both of us realised today that we are essential to each other. I don't want to go away from her."

"I didn't kiss her today, I just wanted to make sure I was good enough for her."

"Her eyes drew me towards her, I couldn't have held myself away from her today. She looked surreal."

And there were more bills from every day that Aarian and I had spent together. I was perplexed and fidgeting through them while tears kept rolling down my eyes.

Then, a hand joined mine, sending the adrenaline bursting through my veins. It was him. Smiling and standing there.

"You think of all the times when your eyes questioned I couldn't understand them? I was just making myself ready to be with someone who deserved everything that was best. I just couldn't gather myself before those eyes that looked at me with so much love that I happened to question myself every time, does this goddess of a woman deserve someone as ordinary as I am?"

His words left me weak in the knees, some doubts remained,"But Trishala? And that diary?"

"I couldn't be surer that I loved you after talking to you about Trishala at the beach. Trishala is my ex-girlfriend. When you talked about happiness all that came to my mind was you and I slogging the night through with your presentation. When you talked about life, all I could picture was your walking towards me with that dazzling smile and everyone turning around to stop and stare at you. When you talked about someone I couldn't let go of, it only reminded of every goodbye that I had to say to you when I left for home. How I wished I never had to say them," he spoke effortlessly, a measure of enlightenment shining through his eyes.

I fell to my knees as a new set of hands helped me up. It was Trishala's turn to speak. "Naina, I haven't seen him more in love, when in Goa he came up to me and told me that he had found his girl. Aarian and I weren't meant to be together. I had a fight with my boyfriend in Goa and when I saw Aarian there, I went all weak. I was too drunk when I met him at the beach. I tried to kiss him but he didn't let me, instead he got me sobered and helped me get back together with Raj. He made me and Raj meet and got things sorted out between us.

"Aarian and I were always best friends and we are happy nurturing that bond again. He talked so highly of you that I really wanted to meet you and so I am here. Moreover my boyfriend is here too, he thought all four of us would go on a double date but I didn't know this idiot had not yet formally offered his heart to you," said Trishala, now enveloping me in a hug."And about the letter…" she began, but handed me the diary instead. It was the same diary from which Aarian had been reading out to her. I started from where I had left.

I love you! I love you a lot! If it wasn't for the beaming light of that truck, if it wasn't for Divya's abrupt presence, if it wasn't for a voice inside me shouting that she deserves the best and you are just another guy, I would have kissed you every time the universe offered a perfect setting to bring us together. I cannot think of anything beyond you, Naina. That day during our walk when the moon shone on your bright pink flawless face I asked myself, could this goddess of a woman ever love me? During that sunset when your hair danced with the wind, I wondered if the sea looked better or you? Of all the times your magnetic charm drew me to kiss you I only restrained myself for what I read in your eyes was not consistent with what went on in my head. Someone as idyllic and impeccable as you couldn't be falling for me? Please end my turmoil and suspense today Naina! I love you...

Was all this real? I wanted someone to pinch me and tell me I wasn't dreaming. I had lost my words until Shabana came up to me and declared, *"Didi aapka brufin ro rha hai,"*(sister, your boyfriend is crying) and I heard everyone laugh. I looked around to see Kritti, Isha, Vinay, Uttara and Divya standing there giggling.

Aarian was there too, looking at me with love in his eyes and tears that yearned for me. I rushed and hugged him. The moment our bodies met, I closed my eyes and became oblivious to the people around me; I hugged him and cried. I wept uncontrollably. And this time, gushing with happiness.

"I love you so much you ass! I have loved you since always! And don't you call yourself an ordinary man now, you are my prince charming!" I said overwhelmed.

He was mine now. It wasn't anymore about me or him, it was about us. I kissed him and I heard something play in the background, 'Everything I do, I do it for you'. Kritti, Isha, Vinay, Uttara and Divya stood there singing with wide-ass grins.

My perfect kiss with this song sung by my best friends in the background; I could not have asked for more. I looked at the sky and smiled at Niti, she was the one with whom I would discuss my perfect kiss, my perfect make out. Ya that too. I then looked around myself. I couldn't have been happier. It was a moment that calling perfect would have been an understatement. These people constituted my life.

"I didn't know you wrote so well," I said as Aarian held me from behind and everyone else was entering Barista.

"Your rub-off effect, baby!" he declared.

Someone was going to address me as 'baby' from now on! I thought and danced in my head.

That evening, I had the time of my life.

✦ ✦ ✦

Epilogue

I realised that being loved is a feeling that transforms you as a person. It is a feeling of when you realise that there is someone who will wait through the day to catch your glimpse even for a minute. Who will read your silences and be ears to all your nonsense. Who will nag you on being asked to go shopping but on making a cute puppy pout will give up helplessly caressing you in his arms; whose touch would make butterflies dance within you every time, whose fragrance was enough to turn you on, who would go all the way to your metro station to spend a little more time with you but importantly will love you for whatever you are.

It has been a year and Aarian and I are still very much in love. He had gone to New York for his film appreciation course and I have been preparing for my Mass Comm entrances. Thanks to Skype, we never got enough of each other. For reasons more than one! But now that he is back, after a complete year there, we are inseparable. People ask us if we endorse Fevicol.

Kritti and Isha remain the same. Kritti stays by my side unfailingly and is preparing for her MBA entrances; Isha and Mohit carry on their cycle of break-ups and patch-ups.

Divya went back to New York and is still as sexy as ever. We mail each other quite often. She is planning to take up modelling as her career. She says my show at Hindu inspired her.

Uttara and Vinay, needless to say are as much in love as ever. God bless them.

Bhaiya and Manali are happily engaged and the families now sit together for the preparations of their wedding scheduled for late next year. And my brother will marry twice, to the same girl though, once in Kolkata, with all the bong rituals and once in Jalandhar, the typical big fat Punjabi wedding.

Mishti is doing her psychology honours from IP College for women. We live together now, which means the slippers are more in the air than they are on the ground. These siblings I tell you.

Salman and Shabana are doing well. I got them at my home once and made Maggi and coffee for them. We all loved it. The *tapori* dance followed. (I taught them). All five of us often have such parties! That is Me, Mishti, the two kids and Aarian.

Trishala and Raj often drop by us. They are happy and are together. Me, Aarian and they go on double dates often.

Rishab, I guess is alive. That's all I know of him. Like I care?

And the CCD, guy? Oh well, he's the store manager now.

As I still and always will hold on to her memories, Niti, remains in our hearts, alive and still very much a part of me.

And about my life, it goes on happily, very much soaked in love.

I close my story for you by quoting my favourite lines from Emily Dickinson:

I had no time to hate, because
The grave would hinder me,

And life was not so ample I
Could finish enmity.

Nor had I time to love, but since
Some industry must be,
The little toil of love, I thought,
Was large enough for me.

(Emily Dickinson, "I Had No Time to Hate, Because")

✦ ✦ ✦